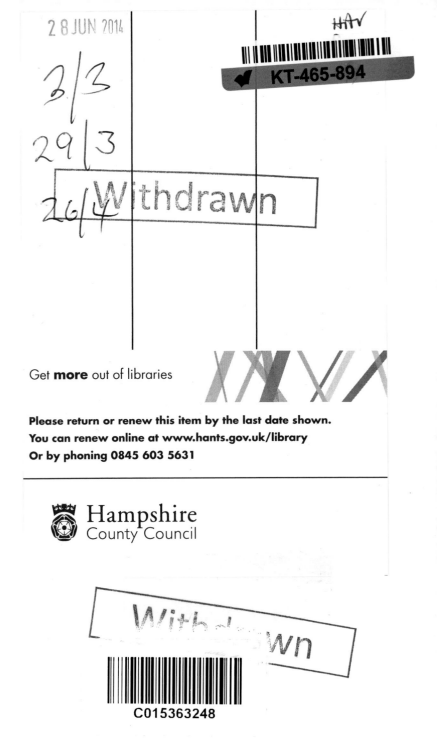

Get **more** out of libraries

Please return or renew this item by the last date shown.
You can renew online at www.hants.gov.uk/library
Or by phoning 0845 603 5631

Hampshire
County Council

'Why don't you marry a husband who'll keep you from roaming the Borders alone?'

Flour still clung to her apron, and he couldn't help but think she looked ridiculous instead of haughty.

'I will,' she said finally. 'Soon. Someone worthy. Special.'

Special. She said the word as if to insult him. 'Who is special enough for you?' The words curdled on his tongue. Why even ask? He didn't care. Not really.

'No one you would know. No one the least bit like you.' She turned away, as if she could choose to end the conversation.

Suddenly he wanted to know who would possess this infuriating woman. 'He interests me if he will ride to rescue you.'

She looked back at him, eyes wide. He was not skilled with women, but this one was hiding something.

'Then you will have to wonder at it, won't you?'

And he did wonder. She was more than of an age to marry, and more than passable to look on. Why was she not yet wed?

And as he looked at her he was also wondering why he had ever thought taking Stella Storwick was a good idea.

AUTHOR NOTE

Black Rob Brunson, oldest son and head of the family, brooded silently at me as I wrote the first two books about *The Brunson Clan*. I began his story with trepidation, not sure I knew what was behind his scowl.

At least I had spent two books with him. Of Stella, I knew no more than Rob did. She was an enemy. And a temptation.

But, ah, the joy of discovery! Is that not the best part of falling in love?

TAKEN BY THE BORDER REBEL

Blythe Gifford

First published in Great Britain 2013
by Mills & Boon, an imprint of Harlequin (UK) Limited.
Large Print edition 2013
Harlequin (UK) Limited, Eton House, 18-24 Paradise Road,
Richmond, Surrey TW9 1SR

© Wendy B Gifford 2013

ISBN: 978 0 263 23274 5

Harlequin (UK) policy is to use papers that are natural,
renewable and recyclable products and made from wood grown in
sustainable forests. The logging and manufacturing process conform
to the legal environmental regulations of the country of origin.

Printed and bound in Great Britain
by CPI Antony Rowe, Chippenham, Wiltshire

After many years in public relations, advertising and marketing, **Blythe Gifford** started writing seriously after a corporate layoff. Ten years and one layoff later, she became an overnight success when she sold her Romance Writers of America *Golden Heart* finalist manuscript to Harlequin Mills & Boon. She has since written medieval romances featuring characters born on the wrong side of the royal blanket. Now she's exploring the turbulent Scottish Borders. The *Chicago Tribune* has called her work 'the perfect balance between history and romance'. She lives and works along Chicago's lakefront, and juggles writing with a consulting career.

She loves to have visitors at www.blythegifford.com and www.pinterest.com/BlytheGifford, 'thumbs-up' at www.facebook.com/BlytheGifford, and tweets at www.twitter.com/BlytheGifford

Previous novels by the same author:

THE KNAVE AND THE MAIDEN
THE HARLOT'S DAUGHTER
INNOCENCE UNVEILED
IN THE MASTER'S BED
HIS BORDER BRIDE
RETURN OF THE BORDER WARRIOR*
CAPTIVE OF THE BORDER LORD*

The Brunson Clan

**Did you know that some of these novels
are also available as eBooks?
Visit www.millsandboon.co.uk**

To all those who face
the tyranny of expectations.

Robin, in thanks for many kindnesses
and the occasional kick in the pants.

And in memory of Marley,
a bloodhound much loved by his family,
who helped me understand the
character of sleuth-dog Belde.

Left on the field by the rest of his clan
Abandoned for dead was the first Brunson man
Left for dead and found alive
A brown-eyed Viking from the sea
He lived to found a dynasty.

Silent as moonrise, sure as the stars,
Strong as the wind that sweeps Carter's Bar
Sure-footed and stubborn, ne're danton nor dun'
That's what they say of the band Brunson

Every Brunson leader since the first knew
his beginnings.

Knew that the blood that coursed through
his veins was shared with the First Brunson,
a man so strong he refused to die.

That was the strength this clan demanded.

Each head man has to find his own within.

Sometimes it was not what he expected...

Chapter One

The Middle March—April 1529

When Black Rob Brunson took his first waking breath that morning, he inhaled air free of the stink of cinders for the first time since the Storwicks had torched the tower's buildings scarce two months before.

Yet his waking thought was the same that morning as it had been the one before and the one before and the one before that. They would pay. Every last one of them.

Oh, he had taken retribution quickly. Their roofs had felt flame. Their head man now languished under the eyes of a Scottish guard.

But it wasn't enough. Not for all they had done.

The ashes had faded with the snow. The kitchen roof had new thatch, but with his second breath, he knew the truth. His nose would never be free of the stench.

Nor would theirs. He'd make sure of that.

He swung his feet over the side of the bed and glanced over his shoulder, still half-expecting his dead father's ghost to lurk behind him.

Nothing there.

Rob was alone in the head man's chamber. He was the head man now, as he'd been raised to be for twenty-six summers.

He stretched, scratched an itch on his back and reached for his boots.

Snow and frost had lingered, but this morning, he felt a softness in the air. Spring. Lambing time. Time for him to be a shepherd as well as a warrior, riding the valley to be sure the flock was well tended.

Last year, he had ridden beside his father.

Up and dressed, he foraged the kitchen, searching for a leftover bannock to stuff in his bag. His sister used to do that for him, for all of them. Cooked the food, washed and cleaned, kept everything in order until a few months ago, when she deserted them for that untrustworthy husband of hers.

Soon, they'd be harrying *him* to find a wife. Some woman who would fuss at him for riding out alone. Danger was not gone with the snow, but he would be back before dark and no one would dare a daylight raid on a sunny spring day.

Besides, he preferred the solitude. Alone, he'd have at least a few moments when no one was looking at him, waiting for his word to be the final one.

He walked through the gate and surveyed the ponies grazing outside the walls, glad to leave the tower behind. He whistled and Felloun trotted over, ready to ride. In truth, Rob felt more at home on the horse than anywhere else. The ground beneath the pony's hooves, the land itself was home to him. He was part of it—hills, moss, rocks and soil. Kin to the earth, he sometimes thought, and not to men at all.

But that was the way of all Brunsons, since the First. A Brunson was of the land. Of *this* land.

The other half of him, the half some men found in mates, that half was in these hills. None would force them asunder.

He reached the closest family before the sun was high. Bleating sheep milled about and a well-trained dog tidied the edges of the flock, responding to his master's whistle.

Rob nodded to the man. 'All well?' Not to suggest Fingerless Joe needed help. Simply to be here if he did.

'Aye.'

A new lamb, wobbly on his legs, stayed close to its mother.

Rob swallowed. 'The little one. Strong enough to move to high land come June?'

The man shrugged. 'He will or he won't.'

Rob looked away, towards hills that blurred before his eyes. It was the way of things. Weakness meant death. For man or beast.

He looked back at Joe, clear-eyed again. 'Any sign of Storwicks?'

Another shake of the head.

'Next week, then.' Rob pushed a knee into his horse's side and the beast turned, obedient.

No sign of them that Fingerless Joe might see. Rob would look for himself.

By midday, Rob was high above the valley where a hoof-worn track wound across the hills and over the border, one he knew well.

As did the Storwicks.

He rode across the border and back, looking for fresh horse droppings.

The path was clear, so he returned to his side of the hill, dismounted, stretched out on the ground and gazed down on the valley that was his. Clear, this day. Clear as he'd seldom seen. He could see all the way to the tower, thrusting up strong from the greening grass.

Tempting to a Storwick, aye, but there was no weakness there. Not now.

Something shifted. The wind. A scent. A sound. He stiffened, alert, and turned his head.

Above him and to his left, sat a woman, silent and stiff, eyes fixed on him warily as if he were a Storwick.

He fashed himself for not looking carefully before leaving his horse. What if he'd been surprised by the enemy?

Neither spoke, looking.

Dark hair tumbled across her shoulders, but he would not call her beautiful. At least, not from this angle. Eyes and lips fought for control of her face. Her nose was too strong. Her chin too sharp. She looked vaguely familiar, but he had seen every far-flung Brunson at one time or another. Still, he could not summon which branch of the family was hers.

'You're far from home,' he began, still trying to place her. The Tait cousin lived nearest, but he had no daughters.

She drew herself up into a crouch, like a wary animal ready to run. 'Nay so far.'

He raised and lowered his shoulders, sorry he had frightened her. He motioned his head uphill, towards the border. 'Storwicks are no more than five miles away.'

Not taking her eyes from his, she stood slowly and took a step back, as if nearness to the enemy had just occurred to her. The blush on her cheek paled. 'Have I crossed the border then?'

'Nay.' He rose to his feet, uncomfortable that she stood while he was stretched out on the grass. What was the strangeness in her accent? 'It's just over there.'

Her eyes widened. She turned to look over her shoulder. Then ran.

That was when he recognised her.

* * *

Stella Storwick didn't look back, praying for her feet to run faster.

But the Brunson kept coming, strong as a charging ram, trampling the grass behind her. Then he was in front of her, cutting off her escape as if she were no more than an unruly ewe.

She dodged. Left. Right. Thinking she could confuse him.

He was a broad man. She could be quicker. More steps, her skirt and the grass holding her back. If she crossed the border, she would be safe…

But next she knew, he grabbed her arm, whirled her around and both of them tumbled to the ground. She on her back, pressed to earth, he straddling her legs.

She lifted a clawed hand to scratch his eyes, but he caught her wrists and held her arms tight against the dirt without effort. Even when she shut her eyes against him, he surrounded her, warm and smelling of leather.

'You're Storwick.' He did not ask a question.

She opened her eyes. His were brown. And murderous.

'And you're Brunson.' Close now, she knew him, the man she had seen near half a year ago at Truce Day. Fool she was, not to have recognised him immediately.

Not just *a* Brunson. *The* Brunson.

A flash of heat crackled through her body. Hatred, no doubt.

He was one of the Black Brunsons. Broad of shoulder and brow, dark of hair and eye. Yes, he had the brown eyes that marked all his cursed clan.

'You'll not take me.' She braced herself, stiff armed and legged, as if that would stop him. 'I won't let you.'

He froze, then turned to spit in the dirt in contempt. 'Brunsons don't treat women so.' Disgust now, in his eyes. 'It's your kind who do that.'

One villainous kin of hers who had done that.

She knew the truth of the whispers about him, though the man had never dared touch her.

No one dared that.

'That's not what I've heard.' A lie, but one she hoped would keep him off guard. She tugged against his hold. An iron manacle would have given way more easily.

He released her hands with a look that warned her to keep them quiet. 'You've heard wrong.'

She pushed herself up on her elbows. 'Then let me go if you don't mean to take me.'

He sat back on his heels and crossed his arms, his very silence ominous.

She held her breath to stop her speech. He had not guessed *which* Storwick she was. Or that she had come to the hills to spy on his precious tower.

'How far behind are the others?' He stood, pulling her to her feet, keeping his hand on her wrist while he gazed towards the English side of the border.

'No others.' Foolish admission. She had told no one her plan when she left this morning. Perhaps that had been unwise.

He turned back, sweeping her with a glance head to toe. One that said she might be daft, but he wasn't. 'You wander the hills alone with no horse?'

She shrugged to hide the shaking. 'Sun doesn't often come like this. I wandered too far.' And had hoped to wander further. A horse would draw attention. 'Let me go. I'm of no use to you.'

'Oh, you're of use to me. You're going to serve as a hostage for the good behaviour of the rest of your people. If they ride to rescue Hobbes Storwick, you'll be the one to pay.'

She blanched. Thank God. At least her father was alive.

They had not even been sure of that.

In violation of the Border Laws, the Brunsons had torched her home and captured her father, too ill to travel to the most recent Truce Day gathering.

But never too ill to defend his home.

Since then, there had been no word. None of them would have put it past the Brunsons to have killed him outright, but if he was alive, who held him?

That was why she had come to the hills today. To discover if her father was alive, where and what it might take to rescue him.

At his words, he'd seen a flash of fear disrupt the pride in her eyes. As if she really thought he was no better a man than her own vile kin.

Scarred Willie Storwick had shown no mercy to Johnnie's Cate. This woman deserved no better.

But Rob Brunson was not a Storwick.

He sighed and eased his grip on her arm. The road to the south was clear and quiet, but he wondered whether to trust his ears and eyes. He'd been so lovesick at the sight of his land, he had not even noticed her before he dismounted.

His father would have never made such a mistake.

Against her skin, his palm heated, but he could not let her go or she would run again, bringing the others if they were not already on the way.

'You're a Storwick, that I know.' He remembered, too late, why she looked familiar. He had seen her on Truce Day, last autumn, and spared one glance too many for her swaying hips. 'Which one?'

She lifted that pointed chin in his direction, then pursed her lips before she answered. 'One of the Red Storwicks.'

A Red Storwick without red hair, but she had the green eyes, huge and heavy-lidded. 'You're looking at Black Rob Brunson,' he said.

She nodded, as if the news were old. 'I know. Head of your clan.'

She could say so, but after eight months, those

words still did not come easily to his tongue. 'What do they call you?'

'Stella.' No hesitation this time.

'What kind of name is that?' It was no name he had ever heard. Not like Mary or Agnes or Elizabeth.

One she was proud of, judging by the way she held her head. 'It's Latin.'

'Latin! Only churchmen know that.'

'My mother does.'

Disbelief must have shown clear on his face.

'Well, she knows a word or two.'

Proud of that, too. This woman seemed proud of everything. 'So what does it mean, your name?'

'Star.'

A chill rippled down his back. *Silent as moonrise, sure as the stars.* Thus began the Ballad of the Brunsons.

Those stars had no connection to this woman. None.

'Well, Stella Storwick, you'll have no need for Latin in Brunson Tower.' He pointed to the pony. 'Up there. Now.'

Stella kept her head down as they rode through the Brunson gate, hoping he would not see how closely she studied the family stronghold. Would they hold her father on the top floor? Or in the tower's dark bowels? She searched every slit in the stone wall, hoping to see his face.

Black Rob rode behind her, his arms reaching around her, tight as shackles, to hold the reins. After he dismounted, he helped her down, a greater kindness than she had expected. Men appeared. A few women. A young, round-faced boy stared at the head man as if he were a hero.

Someone led the horse away and Rob told them who she was in few words while she looked around. The Brunsons had made more progress on rebuilding since their last raid than the Storwicks had.

Of course, they'd had more time.

He pushed her ahead of him towards the tower.

'Where are you taking me?'

'To the well room with the ale barrels,' he growled. 'And the spiders.'

Her heart beat faster. *No, please not there*. She swallowed.

He studied her silence. 'Afeared?'

Stella stood straighter. 'No Storwick ever feared a Brunson.'

'The canny ones did.' No touch of sympathy warmed the cold words.

'Is that where you hold Hobbes Storwick?' If so, she would force herself, despite the fear.

He narrowed his eyes and stared at her until she felt certain he knew who she was and why she asked. 'No,' he said, finally.

Did that mean they did not hold him in that room? Or was her father not here at all? She wrestled her disappointment.

Inside, thick walls blocked the sun. Cool, damp air, smelling of ale, surrounded her. And she heard the echo of water, deep in a well…

Once safely ten steps beyond the sound, she breathed again. She was to be spared that, at least. For now. With the reprieve, she could think again and realised she had been walking since daybreak.

At the tower's next level, she paused. 'I need…' She faced implacable disgust in his eyes. He would not care that she needed a garderobe and a moment of her own. It was not something she wished to speak of to any man.

Remember who you are, Stella.

She lifted her head and fixed her stare on Black Rob. 'I need time for women's things.'

Puzzlement, then understanding unseated the disgust in his eyes. A flush stained his strong cheekbones. Still gripping her arm, he pushed her to the other corner of the floor until they stood before the door of the little room. The man who had been full of bluster shifted from one foot to the other.

A young girl walked out of the hall and he dropped Stella's arm to grab hers. 'You. Stand before the door. Call me when she's done.'

He stepped back. 'And don't think about jumping out.'

She raised her eyebrows. 'How daft do I look?'

'Daft enough to wander alone on the wrong side of the border.'

She closed the door on him and listened to his retreating steps, grateful for a moment alone to gather her strength. She had planned to get close to the tower, close enough to see or hear something about her father that would force her squabbling cousins to act. Instead, she was within the walls and a prisoner.

If she told Rob Brunson who she was, once he

knew she was Hobbes Storwick's daughter, the man would no doubt take her directly to her father and then…

She sighed. No. Her first instinct had been the right one. The less they knew of who she was, the safer she would be.

But since she was inside the tower, she could discover where her father was being held. She would see him soon. It couldn't be that hard. Search the floors, speak with a servant…

But what if her father was not here. Then what?

Waiting for the women to return, Rob sat in the Hall, looking out over the valley, and argued with himself. He had felt her flinch when he mentioned the cellar, yet a Storwick man deserved no better than the laich level. Nor a Storwick woman, either, but he couldn't shake that memory of her expression, a strange mix, as if she were frightened, but too proud to admit it.

Never show weakness, son. Especially not to a Storwick.

No doubt this woman's father had said near the same.

The Tait girl brought Stella into the Hall and

he looked at her eyes, deeply, for the first time. Green, they were, and shadowed with strong brows that gave her a slightly disapproving look.

Well, she'd have no reason to disapprove of her treatment by the Brunsons. At least not until she earned worse. She was, after all, a woman and he was not a cruel man, though his enemies had been known to disagree.

'We've an empty room,' he said, as he led her to the next level. 'It will be yours for now. But the minute you try to escape, it will be down to the cellar with you.'

He opened the door and she stepped in, turning to survey the room. 'A bit barren, but it will do.'

'Barren?' He was still unused to the luxury of the curtained bed he'd been sleeping in these last months. This room had a broad bed, fireplace, and stool. What more did a body need? 'It was good enough for my sister. Unless you'd prefer the cellar.'

He thought she flinched again, but just as quickly, her calm returned. 'No. This will do.'

'Do?' The word a judgement. 'You should be

grateful I'm letting you set foot in my sister's room.'

A pout seemed to threaten her lower lip. 'It's just…it's not what I'm accustomed to.'

'Are you accustomed to one of your English king's castles, then?'

Her eyes widened, neither fear nor insult in her gaze. 'I'm not accustomed to the Scots side of the border at all.'

'Easy to tell. You don't even know where it is.'

'I do now,' she snapped, taking his eyes square.

Was that warning or temptation in her green gaze? No matter, he met it, refusing to waver. 'Next time, stay on your own side.' He turned his back and reached for the door, but she called to him before he could close it.

'I would. If only the Brunsons would do the same.'

He pulled the door closed. Hard.

Chapter Two

As the door slammed behind him, Stella realised that her heart had somehow galloped up to her throat. Closing her eyes, she put a hand to her chest, trying to slow its beating and move it back to its proper place.

Aye. This man, this savage Brunson, was all they had ever said of the clan. And more.

God saved you, her mother always said. *You are special in His eyes and He will let no harm come to you.*

She opened her eyes to look around the room again, wondering whether God's reach extended to this godless side of the border.

Capture had not been her plan when she left home this morning. Truth of it, she had no plan, but she could take no more of the endless bickering between Humphrey and Oswyn. Her father was ill and in Brunson hands. She had to do something.

Beneath her hand, her heart settled into a steadier rhythm.

She'd been spared the cellar, which meant his intention was to ransom her. In the interim, as custom decreed, she would be treated as a guest.

Yet they had asked no ransom for her father, as would have been expected. Did that mean he was already dead?

Something hit her door, too close to the floor for a knock.

She jumped and her heart thumped in answer.

The sound came again, on the floor this time, in an irregular rhythm. She opened the heavy wooden door and looked out.

The blond, round-faced boy she had seen in the courtyard ran up and down the hall, kicking a ball. When he saw her, he let the ball roll away.

'Gudday,' she said, noticing no one else was in the hall. No guard, then. Perhaps God's will did extend so far north.

'Gudein, lady.' The boy mangled the words, as well as the time of day.

Still, she smiled. Children always made her smile. 'What do they call you, lad?'

'Wat,' he said, his smile widening to meet hers. 'I be Wat.'

She looked again, more carefully. A simpleton, by the sound of him, perhaps eight or ten. And one who knew the Brunson buildings better than she.

'And I'm Stella.' Swallowing her guilt, she knelt down, as if taking the boy into her confidence, and laid a gentle hand on his shoulder. 'Wat, can you show me the tower? I'm sure I would get lost by myself.'

This might be her only chance to search for her father. And surely even Rob Brunson couldn't fault a brainless boy for helping her.

Wat threw an uncertain look over his shoulder, as if hoping for reinforcements.

She squeezed his shoulder, driven by her own urgency. 'I bet you know the best hiding places. Would you show me?'

Silent, he nodded, took her hand and led her up the stairs.

The warm, sunny day must have lured everyone outside, for they seemed to have the tower to themselves. And by the time she had seen everything from the stone flag roof to the entresol stacked with foodstuffs, she knew there could only be one place left.

Is that where you keep Hobbes Storwick?

No, he had said. But with a pause. A moment's hesitation before a lie?

She looked down the stairs. Somewhere down there, the well's open maw waited.

'Wat,' she said, gripping his hand so that he could not wander into harm's way. 'Show me the well room.'

Late in the afternoon, Rob returned home for the second time that day. After he had left the Storwick woman at the tower, he and his men had ridden hard and far, searching for signs that the Storwicks were riding. He found none. In fact, the family had been strangely quiet since their leader had been taken.

Why?

He had expected an attempt at rescue, or at least retaliation. Instead, only the whine of the wind swept over the border from the English side.

And instead of thinking about the potential threat, he was thinking of her.

Only because he must decide how to notify the Storwicks that she had been captured, not because he was remembering the heat of her, trapped between his legs and the ground.

He forced his thoughts to the simple things. Stabling Felloun instead of leaving him to graze. Removing the horse's saddle and blanket. Fetching his feed. Patting his withers as thanks for another day of service.

With the horse cared for, he pushed open the iron yett that protected the sole door to the tower. Inside, the sound of unfamiliar footsteps echoed from the lower level.

Drawing his dagger, he bent his knees and followed the sound.

'Show me.' A woman's whisper.

Hers.

He stepped more softly.

Back to him, clutching Wat by the hand, she stood peering into the well room. The iron grate had swung open, but she did not step inside. Instead, she leaned in, looking to the corners, as if the threshold itself were a cliff.

He straightened and released a breath, without sheathing his dagger. Well, now he knew he would have to waste a man to guard her door. 'Did you change your mind, then?'

She jumped, gasping, and grabbed the boy close with both hands.

What was she looking for?

He stepped closer, ducking his head to avoid the low ceiling. In the cramped space, his shadow loomed over them. Small, high window holes let in scant late daylight.

'Don't hurt the boy.' Yet she clutched his head to her skirt, tight enough to smother the lad.

'Hurt him?' No more than he would hurt a dumb animal. 'What do you take me for?'

'A Brunson.'

What she thought an insult, he found a compliment. Yet he needed no halfwit, open-mouthed boy under foot right now. 'Wat. Find your mother.'

The lad smiled at Stella Storwick and then ran up the stairs.

Rob moved closer, close enough that it seemed he must take her arm and turn her to look again into the small, dark room. In the centre, a covered well waited patiently for time of siege. Most days, they drew their water from the stream outside the walls.

'So do you favour this instead of the "barren" room upstairs?' The anger in his voice was for himself, but she would not know that.

Shoulders hunched, she shook her head without taking her eyes from the well. Even her silence angered him, making him speak as roughly as she expected. 'Speak to me,' he ordered. 'Do you?'

At that, she stood straight and tall again. 'No.'

One pride-filled word. But had he seen fear, too?

He pushed her ahead of him up the stairs. 'Then stay where I put you.' Her hair swung to one side, exposing the pale skin at the curve of her neck and releasing a scent faint as bluebells. 'Next time, I'll let you stay in the cellar.'

She threw a look over her shoulders, but it was too dark to read her eyes.

They walked the stairs in silence. Already, he regretted the impulse that had made him grab her and bring her home this morning. Once she had crossed into Brunson land, he had no choice, but then he had taken pity on her. Spared her the cell and put her in a room fit for honoured guests, a weakness he would not show again.

He pushed the heavy wooden door open. 'Inside.'

She searched his eyes, then, not answering.

Uneasy under her gaze, he motioned her in. 'Go on, now.'

'Do you hold Hobbes Storwick here?'

Looking for the man. That's what she had been doing. 'I told you he was not down there. Did you not believe me?'

'Does he still live?'

He opened his mouth to reassure her and thought better of it. The truth would be good enough.

'He did when I saw him last.' Few enough of his family had asked whether the man lived or died. 'Now? I can't say.'

Disappointment swept through her, sharp as a Cheviot wind, as Rob Brunson closed the door behind him.

He's not here. He may not even be alive.

The man is a Brunson, hope argued. *Would he keep the truth to himself?*

She and the boy had searched the tower from

roof to ground. She might have missed a corner or two, but not one large enough to house a
prisoner. Still, there were outbuildings.

A window beckoned and she looked down at
the courtyard. The kitchen hugged one wall, the
public hall the other. Unless there was a separate
room carved out of the hall, neither would hold
a prisoner. She had only glimpsed the courtyard
on the opposite side of the tower, but it seemed
even smaller. She remembered only a small
stable and a few huts for storage.

Would Black Rob Brunson be so cruel as to
house a sick man in a hut?

Aye. She had no doubt of that. But then he
would know whether her father lived or died.
And while Black Rob Brunson was many things,
she did not think him a lying man.

No. Her father was not here. She would have
heard something. Even felt something.

Then where, Stella asked herself, as gloaming
settled over the valley, had they taken Hobbes
Storwick?

Cold, tasteless soup had appeared at her door
that evening, swill not fit for hogs, so by late

morning the next day, anger and hunger played tug of war.

Hunger was winning.

The rumble in her stomach made it hard to think, but if her father was not here, then she could do little but wait to be ransomed. But before she left, she would gather some information to take with her.

Everyone knew that the Brunsons could muster more men than any family on either side of the border. Two hundred horse seemed to appear in an instant. More than that when needed. But it was never clear how many of the men were in residence and how far the rest must travel.

Now that she had searched the place, she was sure there were fewer within the tower than they had thought. What else could she learn?

Stella had scant acquaintance with weapons and fortifications. Still, if she roamed the tower and studied carefully, she could describe the details to men who *would* understand them.

She went back to the courtyard window, this time assessing defences, not places to hold prisoners. In the months since the last raid, the Brunsons had rebuilt most of their outbuildings.

And when she had entered the tower, she noted new stone bordering an opening above the door. A gun hole?

Everyone knew no Scot would touch a gun since the second King James was killed by his own cannon, but Rob Brunson did not seem the sort of man to fear a hagbut, if he chose to fire one.

If the Brunsons had guns in large numbers, the Storwicks needed to know it. And if she could bring the news, well, this might be the thing she had been saved to do, all those years ago.

Stay where I put you. Well, Rob Brunson was going to be angry with her again.

Outside the door, she heard the thump of Wat's ball again and smiled. Was there a guard at the door? If so, she hoped he was more malleable than Rob. At home, she had no trouble handling such men. It took no more than a raised brow or a turn of the head and they would step aside, or run to fetch what she wanted. Things might not be so easy here.

But when she opened the door, Wat himself extended a straight arm and a flat palm to block her from crossing the threshold. 'Gudein,' he said.

Evening or morn, if Wat was her only guard, this would be easier than she thought. She took a step forwards, but his arm did not waver. 'May I pass, please?' Surely he only played a child's game.

He shook his head. 'Laird says you stay.'

But Rob Brunson was not in sight. Wat could not stop her, but he might raise a cry if she crossed him. 'The laird meant that this room was to be mine. Not that I could never leave it.'

God would forgive her the lie. It was for a good purpose.

Wat shook his head, fast enough to make himself dizzy. She sighed. Logic seemed wasted on this poor soul, more so than on most children. 'It will be all right,' she said, laying a tender hand on his shoulder and kneeling so her eyes could be level with his. Taking his chin in her fingers, she forced him to look at her. 'You will see. I'll tell him you conveyed his wishes.'

And that was when she saw the mug and the

plaid on the floor. So, Rob Brunson no longer trusted her to stay in her room.

'Guard coming.' He pumped his arm, waving his flat palm at her as if she were an unruly hound. 'Stay.'

Her gaze swept the corridor. She listened for feet on the stairs. She did not have much time. What could she say so that the boy would allow her to leave? 'But I'm hungry. Can you show me where I could find something to eat?'

'Food later.'

She wrestled with her temper. It was not the lad's fault, but talking to this poor simpleton was little better than talking to a stone.

A clatter from the floor above. The real guard on his way, no doubt.

A whisper, then, as if taking the boy into her confidence. 'Black Rob Brunson is your laird, is he not?'

Finally, a wide smile. 'Aye.'

'And you want to be sure he knows everything he needs to know, don't you?'

A nod, with no suspicion now.

She must hurry if she was to send the boy off for the head man before the real guard returned. Wandering the stronghold alone no longer seemed to be an option.

She whispered, urgent and quick, 'Then tell him that I want to speak to him. Now.'

Creases in his forehead showed how hard the task might be.

'Tell him,' she said, 'that I command him to come to this room. Now go.'

She pushed Wat towards the stairs. He scampered away as footsteps approached from above. Quickly, she retreated to the room, closing the door behind her, hoping the boy had not seen her fingers shake.

'She said what?'

Rob realised when Wat cringed that he had yelled loud enough to make the child think the anger was for him. For Sim Tait, yes, who couldn't hold his piss long enough to stand guard for an afternoon, but not for this unfortunate bowbart.

His outburst seemed to have stolen the boy's speech.

'It's all right, Wat.' He put both hands on the boy's shoulders. He could barely understand the child, who seemed to chew each word before he could spit it out. He might have misunderstood. 'Tell me again what she said.'

Wat's eyes searched the ceiling as if the words he struggled to find might be in the rafters. 'Storwick command you to come. Now!'

Imperious words, if they were truly hers.

'Hungry!' Wat yelled.

Rob sighed and shook his head, unable to tell whether Wat or his prisoner was the hungry one.

Truth told, he was new to all this. Until less than a year ago, he had ridden at his father's side, but when Rob took over the role he had prepared for all his life, he had *not* been prepared for a woman prisoner. Particularly not this one.

You can have no weakness, son.

What kind of woman was she? He mulled it over again as he climbed the spiralling stone stairs.

Storwick commands. Not in *his* house.

He quickened his steps and with a withering glance at Sim Tait, pounded on the door, not waiting for permission before he opened it.

She stood before him with a smile and a lifted chin. 'Enter.'

One word. Arrogant as if he had interrupted something and she was graciously giving him permission to do so.

Command you to come. Had she been so bold? Only if she were accustomed to command.

He grabbed her arm and shook it, wishing he could shake her certainty. 'You're not a Red Storwick. You're of Hobbes Storwick's family.'

The high and mighty lift to her chin did not waver, but fear crept into her eyes again. 'What makes you think so?'

'You rode with him the day Scarred Willie escaped.' It came back clearly now. In the midst of a standoff between Brunson and Storwick, she had dismounted to wander the market booths and shop for ribbons. Disobedient, daft and damn distracting. 'And you've done nothing but ask of him since you got here. What kin are you? Tell me.'

'You're hurting me.'

He dropped her arm as if it were on fire.

Silent, she pursed her lips and clasped one

hand to the other elbow, as if to keep it away from the spot he had touched.

Force was what he knew best. Not a good weapon to use against a woman. He shrugged. 'Not surprising you deny him.' He looked away. 'That you're ashamed to admit it.'

'Where is he?' Now she reached for him, fingers teasing his arm. 'Please tell me.'

His lips parted to answer her.

Don't be a weak fool, son.

He'd be damned if he was going to tell her more. They had kept his whereabouts secret for good reason. If the Storwicks knew Carwell had their leader locked tight in his moated castle, a raid would be sure to follow. He pulled his arm away. She was some kin. What difference did it matter which? 'You sent the boy for me. Why?'

'He didn't tell you?'

'A fool's words. Meaningless.'

She looked at him as if wondering whether to say the truth. 'I am hungry.'

Hungry. So the boy had meant her.

'Do you mean,' she continued, 'for me to starve?'

He wanted to lock her in the room so he would

see as little of her as possible, but that meant sending the Tait girl up with food, as if the woman were an honoured guest, entitled to be waited on and to eat a private supper.

But he'd not be accused of cruelty.

The smell of the midday soup, about to be served, crept into the room. Better to keep watch on her. 'We'll be taking food now. Come if you are hungry.'

He jerked his head towards the door and she glided ahead of him, lifting her skirts and floating down the stairs, leaving him to follow as a lackey to a queen.

Her hips and her hair swayed in opposite directions, and once again, he glimpsed the nape of her neck. As quickly, it was hidden behind a curtain of curls, black as his own. What would it taste like, her skin on his lips…?

His foot hit the floor at the end of the stair, jarring him from the vision. He pointed ahead. 'Here.' As if she could not see the hall before them with her own eyes.

She paused at the door, looking over the room, full of wary men.

'Do you expect them to bow?' He pulled on

her arm, more roughly than he had intended. 'Come. Sit.'

The Tait girl set the fare before them. Soup and bread and cheese.

Next to him, Stella took a sip and crinkled her nose in judgement.

'We don't eat banquets here,' he warned. His father ate plain food, though not quite *this* plain. 'I don't care much for comfort.'

Now she was the one who scoffed. 'That's evident. Is there no salt or spice?'

Truth to tell, he thought the soup had lacked since Bessie left, but he did not know how to fix it. 'Could you do better?'

'Depends on the state of your larder.'

His stomach churned. He had more important things to do than count eggs. 'I'll let you find out. You be the cook tomorrow.'

He had no doubt she would find the larder wanting.

Stella took another sip. The Storwick men would be roaring if they had to choke down this swill, but she knew nothing of how to fix better.

God spared your life, her mother always said. *He did not intend for you to spend it cooking.*

The problem was, no one seemed to know exactly how He *did* intend for her to spend it.

'How many men need feeding?' She glanced down, as if the number were unimportant, gripping the bowl of soup so her fingers would not shake.

He shrugged. 'Twenty.'

No more than at home. At least in the tower. 'And the others?'

'Ye needn't worry about more. There'll be no feasting.'

She nodded, hoping she masked a smile. Twenty men. And now she'd be allowed to leave her room to roam the buildings. 'How many girls will be helping me?'

She had seen the man hold back words before, but this time, his jaw sagged. More speechless than silent.

He swallowed. 'How many what?'

Storwick Tower was only a little grander than the Brunsons', but somewhere her mother supervised women who toiled to produce food and drink and clean laundry. Stella had never been one of them.

'Girls.' She waved a hand. 'To help me.' Perhaps all they needed was firm direction. If she just told them what she wanted, they would produce it. A fat hen, perhaps. Or a fresh caught fish.

'The Tait girl does it all.'

Now she was the one near dumb. 'One woman does it all?'

'She does now.'

'Now?'

'Now that Bessie is gone.'

The missing sister. Probably fled this illtempered man and this drudge-filled life. 'Where did Bessie go?'

A frown creased his brow. 'You ask too many questions.'

She turned away from his inspection and forced herself to take another sip. One girl to feed all these men. Well, if one girl did it, it could not be that difficult. Anything would be better than being locked in a room and having nothing to eat but saltless soup.

'I agree. I'll do it,' she said, as if he had given her a choice.

But she certainly wasn't doing it for Black Rob. She just did not want to starve before she assessed his defences and went home.

Chapter Three

After the meal, Rob stomped down the stairs, frustration in every step. Unable to spend another minute with the Storwick woman, he told Sim Tait to take her back to her room.

And *this* time, to make sure she didn't leave it.

He wanted to see the woman no more.

With each glance, she found him wanting. With each word, she judged his failures. And he had neither time nor care for the opinion of a Storwick. Anger, that was all he felt for her. Nothing more. If there *was* something more, he didn't know what it might be and didn't want to.

His steps slowed as he left the tower and headed to the stables. He would be glad when Johnnie came home. Before his brother had left, their conversations had been strained again. They had quarrelled about something—the King or the warden or raising of cattle. Better that Johnnie and his Cate would have their own place soon.

But it was lonesome, being a head man. Never showing weakness, even when you weren't sure whether you had done the right thing.

Not that he would tell his brother that. But it would be nice to have him back here tomorrow. They could go out and race to mount the ponies, as they used to when they were boys.

Johnnie always won.

Normally, the horses grazed around the tower, but Stella Storwick's appearance had made him cautious and he had brought them within the walls. When he entered the stable, he was surprised to see Widow Gregor's Wat brushing Felloun and muttering something incomprehensible over and over.

He smiled when he saw Rob. 'Gudein, my laird,' he said.

'It's past midday, not eve, Wat.' A waste of breath to correct him. The boy was a simple fool. Who knew how long he had been standing there, rocking back and forth, and brushing the same spot on the horse's withers?

'Careful, lad.' He moved the boy aside. 'You'll rub the beast raw.'

'Can I ride beside?'

'No, Wat.' He wanted no companion right now. Particularly not this babbling boy. 'Go find your mother.'

The lad was the youngest of eight and his mother had few moments to spare for a fool.

Wat gathered his things, then paused at the stable door. 'She's pretty, the lady.'

Rob frowned. 'What lady?' Pretending he didn't know.

'The new lady.'

'Is she now? I hadn't noticed.'

Wat nodded, sagely, as if this were wisdom he could impart. 'Aye.'

The lad's comment seemed an accusation. Rob *had* noticed. And tried not to.

'She's a Storwick, Wat. That means she's as ugly as a dragon inside.'

The boy frowned. 'The way you're as stubborn as a tup?'

He raised his brows. Most men would not be brave enough to insult him to his face, but this boy could not be responsible for what he said, no more than if a dog had been given leave to speak. Wat barely knew the words, let alone their meanings.

Or did he?

'Aye, lad.' The boy watched him with worshipful eyes, but didn't know enough of fear to guard his tongue. Refreshing. 'Very much like that.'

Wat tilted his head, as if he were trying to understand. 'Well,' he said, finally, 'she's a pretty dragon, then.'

He chuckled as Wat left.

A pretty dragon, aye. One whose beauty disguised something deadly.

The Brunson larder, she discovered the next morning, was, indeed, wanting.

The Tait girl was already moving among the pots, toting a sack of flour, measuring it out to start baking bread. When Stella walked in, she looked up, her gaze sullen. 'Why are you here?'

'To see if we can put some decent food on the table.'

A belligerent pout took over the girl's face. 'Nothing wrong with the food.'

'Except that it's barely edible.'

'You think it's so bad?' The girl set the sack down and crossed her arms. 'Cook it yourself, then.'

Stella bit her lip and swallowed. If the girl left her alone here, they would all starve. 'I thought you might need help.'

'From a Storwick?' The girl waved her hands in the air. 'Like you helped with this?'

She looked around the rebuilt kitchen, suddenly noticing the charred floor and the misshapen, half-melted pots. Her people had done this with their torches.

Well, it was no worse than the damage from the flaming brands the Brunsons had lobbed into her home, but bringing a blood feud into the kitchen would not fill her stomach. 'I'm surprised they make you do all this alone.'

The girl's shoulders suddenly sagged, weary. 'I make better ale than bread.'

Another blot on Rob Brunson's shield. This was a woman half-grown, no longer a girl, but not old enough to shoulder all this. Had he no better thought than to make this lass responsible for the whole household?

Not a thought to be shared. 'And the head

man? He has no wife?' She had seen no sign he was married, but her breath seemed to pause, waiting for the answer.

The girl shook her head. 'He's not one for women.'

Stella was not surprised. Women would not have much time for that growling beast, either.

'And are there no Brunson women to help?'

'The mother is dead these two years. The head man's sister moved off to marry that Carwell.' She sniffed, as if she liked the Scottish Warden little better than Stella herself did. 'Johnnie and his bride are building their own tower.' She shook her head and leaned forwards. 'And Johnnie's Cate isn't much for cooking.'

Well, there was nothing for it. She'd have to do with what she'd been given. 'What's your name?'

'Beggy.'

'Well, Beggy, I'll tell you a secret. I'm not much for cooking either.' A child saved by God's hand was, in her family's opinion, destined for more important things than brewing and broiling. She gave the girl's stiff shoulders a squeeze and stood. 'But you and I are going to see if we can make something fit to eat.'

'In that?' The girl looked at her, eyes wide. 'That's fine as a feast gown.'

She looked down and sighed. Her wool skirt was stained already. And she knew little more of washing than cooking. 'Is there an apron?'

Beggy pointed. 'One that needs washing.'

Better than none at all. She tied it on and turned back her sleeves. 'Now, where's the salt?'

'Burnt.' She rummaged on a shelf and held up a small sack. 'This is all that's left.'

When she was taken, she had worried about what the Brunsons might do to her. She had never thought that the blows her family had struck against the Brunsons would now fall on her as well.

More lightly, of course. What was a shortage of salt, after all?

'Well, we'll add spices then.'

The girl looked at her, blankly. 'We ran out before Candlemass.'

'Lamb?'

'A little. Too soon for most.'

'Something from the garden?'

Beggy shook her head. 'Not yet.'

Stella looked around the kitchen. 'Is there nothing left?'

'Carrots. But the laird won't eat them.'

'He won't? Well, then, I guess he'll go hungry.' See how *he* liked it.

Johnnie and Cate arrived near midday. While Cate went to feed her slobbering beast of a hound, Rob and John retreated to the laird's private meeting room and Rob told him about the Storwick woman.

When the tale was done, John lifted his brows, doubtful. 'The King has already named us outlaws. And now we hold an English woman?' He shook his head. 'It won't go well.'

Could Johnnie never just accept his leadership? Rob had wanted agreement, not arguments. He had argued enough with himself already.

'You, of all people, should understand.' Because of Cate, Johnnie had more reason to hate the Storwicks than any of them.

But Willie Storwick was dead now, and much of Johnnie's anger had died with him. 'Carwell has stretched the law by holding Storwick without trial. When they discover you've got the woman, they'll ride again.'

'Let them come.'

Johnnie shook his head. 'You've barely finished rebuilding from the last raid.'

'Rebuilt stronger.' He had higher walls. And doubled the watchers in the hills. They would not be surprised again.

'That won't protect us against King James.'

'King James! King Henry! This side of the border or the other, I care nothing for a man I've never seen.'

Now he saw the worry in Johnnie's eyes. 'I've seen him. Bessie barely escaped from him.'

He shook off the guilt. Bessie had insisted she be the Brunson to plead their case to the King. For all the good it did them. Or the King. 'He has no sway with me.'

'Maybe not, but he's put a price on our heads.'

His brother had come home from court, yes. But he still did not fully understand life here and what a leader must do to protect the family. To survive. Rob did.

'And much has come of that, as you see.' He

spat in disgust. 'Who's to fear him? He's barely more than a bairn. Doesn't dare come himself.'

'He will, Rob. I know him. He will.' John grabbed his arm and shook it. 'He burned a man at the stake in St Andrew's.'

Rob couldn't stop the shiver. A man should die on his pony, fighting. Not burned. Not hanged.

And not in his bed, as his father had.

'Can you not just agree with me for once?'

His brother sat back, and crossed his arms, as if knowing further argument would be futile. 'What *are* you going to do with her, then?'

'Hold her here. And if they try to take Hobbes Storwick from Carwell…' He left the threat unsaid. Couldn't bring himself to say he'd kill a woman.

Storwicks wouldn't know that, though. They'd done worse.

Johnnie looked at him, sharply. 'Take Storwick? From a moated castle? Impossible.'

'I'd expect you to try. If I were the one held.'

Silence. Then a sigh. 'Aye. I would.'

Rob nodded, relieved. It was their own kind of truce.

'Do they know yet that you have her?'

'It's been a day. Two. They know she's gone.' A missing daughter. They'd worry, not knowing whether she had fallen into a ravine, drowned in the river... He steeled his heart.

She was safe and better treated than she'd a right to be, but he was surprised to have seen no signs of a search.

'Well, you can't send a message to Bewcastle.'

He sighed. 'Carwell must do it.'

His stubborn sister had been betrothed to the Scottish Warden at the King's command. Then she had defied her brother to marry the man.

Thomas Carwell had managed to dance on the edge of the Border Laws he was paid to enforce and still not infuriate King James. At least, not until he ignored the King's order that he bring the Brunsons to Edinburgh for hanging.

But still, the King had not removed the man from his office. Not yet, anyway.

'He's still the Scottish Warden. He can send an official message through the English Warden.'

'Who's no friend of any of us since we violated the new treaty. He's not going to like it.'

'Neither do I.' You never knew with Carwell. Reiver one day. English collaborator the next.

Agent of the King the day after that. 'What's to keep him from tattling to the King about it?'

'Bessie.'

He sighed. For all that she was a woman, his sister was steadier than most lasses. He certainly missed having her about the tower. He was not a man who craved comfort, but without her, there had been no one to keep the kettle full and stuff fresh feathers into the mattress.

He wondered what the Storwick woman was doing in the kitchen. Probably scheming to poison him.

'Well, I've saddled myself with the woman. And if they don't know I hold her, it's for naught. Would you go to Carwell Castle to tell him?'

'You'll not go?'

He shook his head. He had not spoken to the man since the Storwick raid. Nor to his sister Bessie. He was not ready to start now. 'Not the time to leave the tower undefended.'

Johnnie eyed him for a moment. 'We could take the girl with us. Give her to Carwell for keeping. She'll be surrounded by a moat and out of your hands.'

'And held beside her father. Together, the two

of them would make an irresistible target.' Based on Stella's questions, they did not know where Hobbes Storwick was held. That could not last for ever. 'If I hold her here, she protects our tower and makes them think before they ride to Carwell Castle.'

To protect the tower. No other reason he was keeping the woman. In truth, he'd as soon be rid of her and her haughty air.

Johnnie rose. 'We'll leave tomorrow. Cate will be happy to see Bessie again.' He paused, waiting.

Rob averted his eyes.

'I'll tell her,' his brother said, finally, 'that you asked of her.'

'Tell her I asked for her recipe for lamb stew.'

Family was all. Protecting it, not loving it.

Love made you weak.

The thought of Bessie's stew reminded him that the Storwick woman was in the kitchen and he crossed the courtyard to see how she fared. Drizzle had dissolved yesterday's sun, along with his good mood, and he began to doubt that today's meal would be any more edible than yesterday's.

At the kitchen door, he stopped.

The room—pots, hearth and floor—was white as if a snowstorm had hit.

And in the midst of it, the Storwick woman clutched an empty sack of flour.

Both women turned to him.

'Take her away,' Beggy shrieked, when she saw him. 'I'd rather cook alone.'

Stella blinked. Rapidly.

Mercy. He had no patience for crying females.

He stepped into the room, sending a puff of flour over his boot. 'What's going on here?'

'First, she let the stew burn. Now, she's spilled half our flour!' Beggy's voice danced on the edge of a scream. 'Get her out of here.'

He took Stella's arm, but she looked back at Beggy. 'I should help you clean...'

'No! Don't help,' the girl said. 'Or there'll be nothing left to eat.'

He pulled Stella out of the kitchen and into the courtyard. 'Did you plan to starve us all?'

'I do not cook at home.'

He stared. All women cooked. Didn't they? 'You were the one who complained of the food!' Criticising the lack of foolish luxuries, of no importance to anyone except to her. 'And you don't even cook?'

'I didn't think it would be so hard.'

'For most women, it isn't.'

'Then why don't you marry a woman who can cook?'

Her words hit as hard as horse's hooves on rock. 'And why don't you marry a husband who'll keep you from roaming the Borders alone?'

She licked her lips, crossed her arms, lifted her chin, all as if to fill the space where there should have been words. But flour still clung to her sleeves and her apron and her shoes and he couldn't help but think she looked ridiculous instead of haughty.

'I will,' she said, finally. 'Soon. Someone worthy. Special.'

Special. She said the word as if to insult him. 'Who is special enough for you?' The words curdled on his tongue. Why even ask? He didn't care. Not really.

'No one you would know. No one the least bit like you.' She turned away, as if she could choose to end the conversation. 'And no one who would interest you.'

Suddenly he wanted to know who would possess this infuriating woman. 'He interests me if he will ride to rescue you. Or if he won't ride as long as I keep you.'

She looked back at him, eyes wide, as if both ideas were new to her. He was not skilled with women, but this one was hiding something.

'Then you will have to wonder at it, won't you?'

And he did wonder. She was more than of an age to marry and more than passable to look on. Why was she not yet wed?

And as he looked at her, trailing white dust from her apron, he was also wondering why he had ever thought taking Stella Storwick was a good idea.

Stella kept her fists tight and her chin high, but her smile stiffened.

He would have to wonder because there was no one. Not yet.

There would be. Some day. It was hard to find

the person good enough to join with a child saved by God.

'Well,' he said, a touch of pride in his voice, 'the woman who marries a head man must be special, too.'

Relieved at the shift from her imaginary husband to his imaginary wife, she rolled her eyes heavenwards. 'The woman who marries you will have to have very special patience.'

'The man who marries you will have to be a saint.'

A saint. Yes. That's exactly the kind of man her parents were looking for.

Her stomach growled, loud enough that Rob looked down. 'Next time, eat what's put before you.'

'Next time, put something before me I can eat.' And dinner would be worse, now that she had singed the stew.

'Brunsons don't whine about food.' He took her arm and pushed her ahead of him. 'I should not have let you out at all.'

She looked towards the gate. He must not lock her in the tower again.

'There ought to be salmon now,' she said,

dragging her feet. Liddel Water was just beyond the gate. Air without walls, a chance to explore, even to escape...

He had retreated to silence and did not glance at her.

She tried again. 'Are you not a fishing man, then?'

Now he looked insulted.

'Ah, I can see that you are not. Because you are such a fighting man.' Maybe she could goad him into it. 'Well, the man who leads the Storwicks provides for their bellies as well as for their protection.'

'We have cattle and sheep to fill our bellies.'

She raised her brows. Her belly, certainly, had not been filled. 'Do you not like fish?'

He paused, as if he were trying to remember the taste. 'I like it well enough.'

'Then why don't you serve it?'

'Not enough salmon to fish.'

'I ate a plateful, only last week. There's plenty of salmon.'

'Plenty for Storwicks because your kind has blocked the cursed stream and the salmon can't get up this far.'

The thought gave her pause. She had known, of course, that her family had built traps that allowed them to feast on fish, but she had never thought about what that would mean for the families who lived upstream.

'Well, we'll have to catch the few there are, won't we?'

'Do ye know any more of fishing than of cooking?'

What she knew about fishing wouldn't fill a leather thimble. But it could not be so hard. Neither was cooking. If the Tait girl had not made her nervous, if there had been unburnt salt… 'I know enough.'

He leaned away so he could meet her eyes. 'Do you, now? Do you know how to build a garth?'

'A what?'

'A garth. A weir, I think you call it.'

'Ah, yes.' She knew the word. It was some kind of construction of sticks that the fish could swim into, but not out of. And she had never touched one in her life.

'Or perhaps the Storwicks spear the fish by torchlight and slaughter them for sport. That would suit your style.'

Had they? Perhaps. They did not tell her all. 'What we don't eat isn't wasted. There's plenty who will pay for good fish.'

'Is that how you pay for those clothes, then?'

She looked down. 'Clothes?' She looked down at her dress, now covered with flour outside the apron's reach. She might have brushed away the flour dust, but now the mist was turning it into white mud.

'You've got sleeves big enough to drag across the table and you're wearing a gold cross fine enough for some king's spawn.'

Without thinking, she touched the cross at her neck. The women of Brunson Tower wore coarse wool, laced vests and tight sleeves, as did most of the women in her home. But her parents had always made sure she had something better. 'A gift. From my parents.'

'Stolen, no doubt.'

'You say that because that's what fills your house.'

They faced each other with stubborn frowns, but there was no answer either could give. Reivers on both sides of the border lived that way.

'There's no disgrace in that,' he said, finally. 'The disgrace is in what else some men do.'

She knew the man he meant. Cousin Willie had been a disgrace to them all. Her father had even disowned him, but somehow the man had become a symbol, a pawn that the English king and warden had blown all out of proportion, leading to raids and treaties and kidnappings, all because of a man hated by his own kin.

Had the Brunsons killed him? Probably.

Was the world better off with him dead? No doubt. But she would not admit that to Rob Brunson.

She drew herself up to her princess height. 'If you are unable, or unwilling, to provide good fresh fish for your table, then say so and I'll go hungry. Don't mock my clothes or insult my family instead.'

Shock. Anger. A clenched fist and jaw and a face as grim as the bare hills in winter. Would his anger be enough for him to let her out of the tower?

'Ye want fish. We'll get fish. But you'll be the one to do it. And I warn you, you and your clothes will be wet and bedraggled before we're through.'

And she couldn't hold back a smile. Because she was sure his would be the same.

Chapter Four

Cate told Rob she couldn't bear to set eyes on a Storwick, so Rob kept Stella in her room until Johnnie and Cate rode west the next morning.

Now, he was left alone with her and with the promise he'd made. He could not force her into the stream wearing a flour-covered dress, so he persuaded a few of the women to loan her skirt, shirt and vest. Stella emerged from the room looking at once like all the other women he knew and nothing like them at all.

Breasts he had barely noticed beneath her own gown now seemed proudly outlined above the Widow Gregor's second-best vest. Beggy Tait's skirt was too short for her, which meant a glimpse of bare ankle. Even the sharp angles of her face seemed softened when she wore ordinary clothes.

But her expression was not.

And still, hanging around her neck was that golden cross, studded with some green stone and with a fleck of flour stuck in the delicate wire. Something finer than he or his father had seen in a lifetime. Her family must have lifted it off the very queen.

But why did she wear it? If Storwick had sold it, his clan could have feasted until the end of days.

Apparently oblivious to the glory around her neck, Stella held out folded fabric, dusted with white. 'I will leave this with the laundress.'

Well, new clothes had taken no edge off her sense of privilege. His anger was exhausted. Now, he was simply baffled. She was no dullard, yet still she surveyed the tower as if she owned it instead of he. 'Do you not yet understand that you are the prisoner here?'

'And do you not understand that I am...?' She let go the rest of the words and her arms, holding the dress, drooped.

'What?'

She shook her head, for once, holding back words.

'No,' he said. 'I don't. Just who *are* you to think yourself entitled to treatment I wouldn't give the King himself?'

Chastened eyes met his. 'I am a hostage for the good behaviour of the rest of my clan.'

He didn't believe she meant a bit of it.

She turned back to the room. 'I'll leave the dress on the bed.'

'Do you know anything more of washing than cooking?'

She looked up, then let her eyes drop as she shook her head.

He sighed. If they didn't clean her dress, she'd have to be garbed in borrowed clothes the others could ill afford to lend. 'Bring it. Widow Gregor does some washing.'

They stopped at the Gregor hut and the Widow's eyes went wide, as if the green dress were as precious as the necklace. 'I'll do my best, but I don't know, I've never...'

Beside him, Stella waved her hand, as if the dress were of no importance. As if she had hundreds more like it at home.

Wat trailed after them as they left, watching Stella with the same worshipful gaze that used to follow Rob.

Truth was, the boy's adoration had never been comfortable for him. It held expectations Rob wasn't sure any man could meet. But he had grown accustomed to it. And it made no sense for the boy to waste his admiration on Stella Storwick.

Wat looked at Rob and smiled. 'She's a *very* pretty dragon.'

Eyes wide, Stella glanced up at Rob, making no apparent effort to hide a smile before she turned to the lad. 'Why, thank you, Wat.'

'Go back, boy,' Rob snarled.

She took the boy's hand and pulled him closer. 'The fault is not his.'

That, he knew. He'd like to make it hers, but that would be a lie. 'We don't need him with us.'

Her hand touched Wat's shoulder. 'He'll do no harm.'

'Nor any good, either.' The boy had few uses. Simple tasks, sometimes, he could do.

'Of course he can,' she said, looking at the

boy as if he were more than a halfwit. 'Can't you, Wat?'

Wat nodded.

'He'll agree with anything you say,' Rob said. Or he used to. Before this woman arrived and the boy developed his own opinions about dragons.

'But *you* told me,' she began, words and eyes sending a warning, 'that he would be good help with whatever we needed.' She hugged the boy closer, as if he were a shield, and the child turned his worshipful gaze back to Rob.

He shook his head. The woman might not be able to cook or wash, but she could manoeuvre this boy as skilfully as he deployed men in battle. And, in the process, she gave him no choice but to be cruel or to allow the lad to come.

He crouched before the boy. 'So you want to fish, do you?'

Wat nodded.

'Then come along.' Under the boy's watchful eyes, he would have to throttle his words. And his temper. Which was, of course, exactly what the woman had intended.

But she was looking at Wat and tugging his hand to draw his attention back to her. 'You must stay close to me and not go too far into the water. I must bring you safely back to your mother.'

But Wat, excited, wiggled like a pup and tugged at Stella's hand, trying to hurry her towards the stream.

'Go, then,' Stella said. Wat took off running. 'But don't go in the water!'

Suddenly alone with her again, Rob missed the boy's protection. 'Well, he's with us. What would you have him do?'

'He can carry the fish.'

Rob threw Stella a warning look. 'If we ever catch one.'

Despite her warning, Wat did not wait at the water's edge, but ran in, stomping and splashing and throwing water in the air.

Stella ran, but Rob was faster. He scooped the wet, wriggling boy from the water and stood him back on the bank. 'Did you think to scare the fish out of the water? If there was a fish there before, he's swum for his life now.'

Wat cringed and Rob realised how harsh he must have sounded.

Stella knelt before the boy and hugged him. 'I told you not to go in yet.'

Wat looked from one to the other and shrugged off her arms, as if bracing for a blow. 'My fault.'

'Yes, it is,' Rob agreed sharply.

Her arms took the boy again and now she was the shield between them. 'Do not blame him. He's a…' She paused, as if not wanting the boy to hear her insult.

'He's a fool.'

'He's a child, not a man.'

'On this side of the border, he is a man. Or should be.' Poor weak creature. Like the baby lamb, destined for an early death.

But her fierce expression brooked no argument.

He put a hand on Wat's shoulder, gently enough that Stella eased her grip and the boy looked up, hopeful. 'Go find us small sticks and twigs, Wat, as many as you can, and bring them back here.'

Reprieved, Wat scrambled down the bank towards the bushes.

'And stay away from the stream,' Stella called after him. 'What will we do with the sticks when he brings them?'

'You know no more of catching fish than you do of the kitchen, do you?' If she was representative of the rest of her clan, it was no wonder they came raiding. Otherwise, they would starve.

'Do you?' She admitted nothing.

He thought for a moment of marching her into Liddel Water to catch the fish alone. She'd be up to those bare ankles in water first. Then, her borrowed skirts would be soaked, clinging to the curve of her hips. And if she were drenched in water the way she had been in flour...

He forced his mind back to the fish. 'Actually, I do.'

She cast a doubtful gaze at the stream, then looked back at him. 'What do I do first?'

He waved his hands. 'Just build a little dam and a place for them to swim in.'

'You've not done this before either, have you?'

'I watched my mother do it.' Watched as she set the sticks in place and relished the luxury of the catch.

'When was that?'

Years. It had been years. 'A while ago.'

'Then how do you know how to do it?'

How? He never asked that question. The *how* of things was passed down in the blood, embedded in the bones. Once the sticks were in his hands, he would remember. 'So you insisted we come out here and build a weir and you know nothing of fishing?'

'I thought *you* knew.'

'Well, in my family, it's the women who do it.'

Shock stole her speech.

He had never wondered at it before. His father had taught him of war and sheep and cattle. The rest was left to the women.

'Well,' she said, finally, 'if you at least had a picture of it, that would help.'

'What do you want?' he retorted. 'A book of lessons?'

'Yes.'

Now he was the one who stared. 'Could you read it?'

She coloured. 'Maybe.'

'Liar.' He was learning her. Without the boy to protect, she had returned to protecting herself.

'I could read a few words.'

'The same two your mother knows?' Just looking at her raised his temper. 'You don't cook, you don't wash, you can't fish...' He waved his hands, fighting the temptation to put them on her shoulders and shake her. 'What are you good for, lass?'

Pink embarrassment crept from her cheeks to the roots of her hair. He had upset her, which was no less than he had intended, but he had not expected to feel guilty for it.

But before she could answer, Wat ran out of the bushes, trailing sticks. He stopped in front of Rob and thrust the pile of twigs and sticks into his arms. 'Here!'

Then he stepped back and looked from one to the other, his face transformed by a proud, happy smile.

Stella crouched before him. 'That's good, Wat. You did a good job. Can you get us some more?'

He nodded and ran off again.

'Children,' she said, gazing up at Rob with a soft smile. 'I'm good with the children.'

Stella watched Rob's scowl turn to frustration. He flung Wat's precious twigs to the ground.

'Then go marry someone special and have some.'

She rose, resisting a sharp answer, and tilted her head to study him. No man—indeed, no one at all—had ever treated her this way. Everyone at home spoke to her carefully, as if afraid to upset or anger her.

As if afraid to evoke any emotion from her at all.

But his words were like a spear in her empty womb.

'When you let me go home, I will,' she said, wishing that words could make it so.

Rob's strong, stubborn gaze turned tender. Aye. Somewhere behind the black brow and the angry words, there lurked a touch of softness. Maybe some day, he'd find a woman who could release it.

'Truce, then.' Two words, but in those, she heard the lilt of a song.

She smiled and nodded towards the water. 'Truce, while we see if between the two of us, we can figure out how to catch some fish.'

They waded into the water and Rob selected a place in the stream to build the dam. She explained to Wat what they needed and he ran back and forth, tireless, heaping twigs upon twigs.

Determined to prove her worth for something, she gritted her teeth, as silent as Rob, and bent to the tedious trial and error of lacing and stacking the sticks so they would not be washed away. At the end of the afternoon, wet, tired, and bedraggled, they had a makeshift weir, ready to trap a passing salmon or two or three.

Wading out of the stream, she sank down on the bank, heedless of the grass and mud beneath her. Rob did the same. Wat, quick to copy, sat between them, looking from one to the other.

'You did well, boy,' Rob said, ruffling the boy's hair.

Wat smiled, bright as the sun.

Then, with a satisfied sigh, Rob stripped off his shirt.

She tried not to stare, but drops of water ran down the curve of his shoulders and traced the muscles of his arms and she remembered the feel of him, holding her to the earth, of that one moment she had no choice but surrender...

She cleared her throat and turned her eyes to Wat. 'Yes, you did.'

'So did you.' The rumble of Rob's voice cascaded through her.

'Can I tell my mother?' Wat said. 'Can I tell her what I did?'

Stella looked to Rob. 'Aye. Go on.'

'She'll be pleased,' Stella called out, hoping it was true. 'I worry about him,' she said, after the boy was out of earshot. 'His mother doesn't seem to have any time for him and it would be so easy for…'

For something to happen.

Rob looked at her, silent.

She lifted her chin. 'Someone should watch him.' She did not want to ask permission. Did not want to say please.

'What? Why?'

So he does not fall into the well.

'Is he not a child of God who deserves to be cared for?'

'He's a halfwit who will never survive without help.'

'Then you admit he needs help!'

A hint of disgust edged his eyes. 'The boy must learn to survive on his own. I did.'

No. This man would not have sympathy for the weak. Strong, bold. He would not understand what it was to doubt.

'But what if he can't?'

'Then he will be better off. If he can't survive childhood, he'll not survive a life on the Borders.'

Maybe he was right. Maybe this child would be better off dead.

Maybe she should have died in that well, too.

'Besides,' Rob continued, 'no one has time to follow a child around all day.'

'I do.'

He studied her face, his still as black as his name, and she thought he would deny her.

'Go,' he said, finally. 'Ask his mother, then. I care not.'

Something, a pull of gratitude, rushed through her, threatening tears. Afraid to look at him, she stared at the sun-dappled water splashing over the little dam of sticks they had created, wishing, violently, that just once, the man would see the world without certainty. 'Together,' she whispered. 'We did that together.'

In just a few hours of peace, Storwick and Brunson had built a weir. What could they build in a year of truce?

She closed her eyes, then opened them and forced herself to look at Rob again, careful to keep her eyes on his face. 'Now all we need is some fish,' she said.

'Oh, soon enough, we'll have fish aplenty,' Rob answered. 'I did not spend the day getting wet and tired to catch a passing carp.'

She studied his face. Sharp cheekbones slanted towards an angled nose, overshadowed with brooding brows and a high forehead. Did he ever smile? 'How can you be so sure?'

'Because by then, the Storwicks' garth is going to be nothing more than sticks floating on Liddel Water.'

Words harsh as a slap jolted her to remember. Black Rob Brunson was no ally, no helpmate. Even a moment of peace was an illusion. Between their two families, there could be no truce.

Not now. Not ever.

Chapter Five

Stella scolded herself, silently, until the sun rose the next morning. She should have known better. She was a prisoner of a cruel enemy. A moment's shared success was nothing more than a distraction

What are you good for, lass?

Nothing, or so it seemed.

Aye, there was the sad truth. She had crossed the border thinking God meant her to find her father and rescue him because her cousins would not. Instead, she had put herself in enemy hands and learned little except that her father was not held in Brunson Tower.

What was she to do now? Care for Wat. That, at least, Rob Brunson had allowed her.

No guard stood by her door, so before she

visited the Widow Gregor, she took the opportunity to wander the courtyard, hoping to see something of use, unsure what she was looking for. She retraced her steps of the first day, looking for something that would speak of the Brunsons' defences instead of a place where her father might be held a prisoner.

She saw nothing that looked materially different from home. If there was something here that would turn the tide of battle, she couldn't recognise it.

Beggy would not let her back in the kitchen. The man in the armoury frowned at her when she paused at the door. Finally, she went up to the parapet, sat on the stone seat near the chimney, and gazed to the south. A man on lookout, standing at the other end of the wall, left her alone.

And looking towards home, she knew again that she was on the wrong side of the hills.

At home, when the sun set, you could watch it. Here, it disappeared behind the hills, hidden and as difficult to see as Black Rob Brunson's feelings.

If he had any.

She should have been mourning her father or scheming to escape or counting dirks in the armoury or at least keeping a watchful eye on Wat. Instead, she was thinking about a stubborn, silent man.

Sometimes when he did deign to speak it was in an accent so twisted she could barely understand the words.

No, she did not want to dwell on how much he filled her thoughts. Only because he was difficult to deal with. Only because he was the largest obstacle in her path. No other reason that just before she drifted to sleep at night she found herself thinking of his strong chest, bared in the sun as they sat on the bank…

At least while they built the weir, he did not ignore her. No, that wasn't it. He did not ignore her. He dismissed her. As if what she wanted was unimportant.

At home, what she asked for appeared. She was treated with a deference she only recognised now that it had vanished. Here, she was no longer special Stella, but only an enemy captive.

'Are you sad, then?'

Wat's voice startled her. How long had he stood there watching her?

Yet he was the one soul in Brunson Tower who looked at her with sympathetic eyes. She motioned him closer. He put a hand on her knee and she ruffled his blond curls. 'Aye, Wat. I'm sad today.'

'Why?'

Because I'm feeling like the Lost Storwick.

What would the poor lad say if she were to tell him how cruel his hero was? But was that true for Wat? She had seen Rob impatient with the boy, yet never cruel.

She pulled him close and hugged him until he wiggled. No. There was no use in making this poor child sad as well. The child seemed too foolish to understand sadness.

Or too wise.

'I was missing my father,' she said, then forced a smile. 'But I feel better when I talk to you.'

'My father is in Heaven.' He smiled, as if Heaven were as close as Canonbie.

'Is he, now?'

He nodded. 'I'll see him there when I die and all the saints and Red Geordie Brunson, too.'

Speechless, she nodded back, wishing she had the kind of faith this boy did. The kind of faith her mother did. 'Red Geordie? That's Rob's father?'

'Aye. He went there and left Rob to care for us here.'

She stifled her observation on how well the head man was doing at the job.

'Come, Wat.' She stood and took his hand. 'Do you think your mother will lend you to me for a while?'

He nodded, swinging her arm. The touch of his trusting hand in hers nearly made her cry. Special, aye. So special that she had never married, would not have children of her own.

She squeezed back and they went down the stairs.

When they entered the small hut at the edge of the courtyard, the Widow Gregor glanced up with eyes that looked one hundred years old.

'What is it?' she said, immediately. 'Wat, did you bother this woman?'

The boy hung his head. She squeezed his hand. 'No,' she answerd quickly. 'Not at all.' Eight

children, Rob had said. And a poor widow saddled with them all. No wonder she had no time
or patience for one who was special.

'Ah, then you've come for your dress,' she said,
picked up the carefully folded green velvet and
handed it to Stella.

'Thank you.'

'I tried me best, but…'

The dress would never be the same. And somehow, it did not matter.

'Come, Wat.' His mother held out her hand.
'Don't bother this lady.'

Stella tightened her hand on his. 'He is no
bother. I'd like to watch him for you.'

Surprise dissolved into relief and then a shrug.
'Do what you like. It will keep him from under
me feet.'

Anger made her tongue tart. 'You take little
enough care of him. He wanders by himself.
Something could happen to him.'

The Widow's weary eyes met hers, a gaze at
once hollow and overfull. 'Who are you to judge
my life?'

No one, she realised. She was no one at all.
'Come, Wat. Find your ball and we will play.'

* * *

Days passed.

Rob allowed her outside the walls, as long as she was with Wat, somehow knowing that the grip of the boy's fingers held her as tightly as an iron chain.

Each day, Stella took Wat down to check the garth, but if there were fish in the river, they were clever enough to swim past the trap. Still, Wat never lost hope.

And she was smiling at his faith when they walked back inside the gates late one morning and she came face to face with the Brunson Warrior Woman.

The woman her kin had so grievously wronged. The woman who had ridden with the men to track him down and exact revenge for the killing of her father.

Beside her, Rob spared barely a glance for Stella. 'This is a Storwick,' Rob said to the woman, not bothering with any other name.

Stella kept a lifted chin high and a wary eye. *Johnnie's Cate isn't much for cooking,* Beggy had said. Wearing pants and boots and a jack-of-plaites vest, but small and fair, she looked nothing like a man. Still, she looked menacing.

'This is Cate,' Rob said, finally looking at Stella. 'Wife to my brother Johnnie.'

'He's in the hall,' the slender blonde said to Rob. 'He wants to see you.'

Rob's hand circled Stella's arm. 'As soon as I lock her upstairs in Bessie's room.'

It seemed her days of freedom had come to an end.

'I'll do it.' Cate drew her dirk and stepped forwards. 'I'd like a word with her.'

He looked from one to the other, then pushed Stella towards Cate.

Stella threw a worried glance at him as he disappeared into the public hall. Cate did not speak again until they reached Stella's room. Once inside, she closed the door and stood in silence.

'What do you want of me?' Stella said, impatience overcoming fear.

'Other than to rip your heart out?'

She shivered, thinking this woman could actually do it. 'Yes, other than that.'

Cate raised her eyebrows. 'What I want is to

see if Storwick women are as monstrous as Storwick men.'

'Well, I'd like to know the same about Brunson women,' Stella retorted.

'Rob? He's strong and hard. A head man must be. But he's no monster.'

Stella sniffed in disbelief. Her father was not so hard, at least, she had never seen him so except with Scarred Willie.

Cate stepped closer.

Stella recoiled.

'I won't hurt you,' Cate said. 'I promise. I know enough of hurt.' Something haunted her eyes.

Stella had heard the women whisper. This woman had suffered at Willie Storwick's hands. 'We heard he was dead,' she said.

Rumour was that the Warrior Woman herself had killed him. If so, no one begrudged her.

Cate blinked, but did not ask who had said this. 'No one has found his body.'

Stella looked at her face again. Aye, she could believe this woman would kill. What would her own life have been like, if she had not been shielded?

'No one mourned him,' Stella said. 'He had been disowned.'

They all knew, the Storwicks, what kind of man he had been. They had learned, too late, how to protect their own from him. At first, her father had threatened him, thinking he would stop and, at first, it seemed as if he had. It was only later, too late, when they discovered he had only taken himself across the hills.

'Truly?' Cate looked sceptical. 'We had heard, but…' She shrugged, as if a Storwick could not be trusted.

'He was no longer Storwick.' Not after Truce Day, when she saw him force a kiss on this Brunson woman and then ride free. After that, her father had cast him out, shunned him and insisted the rest of them do the same. 'Did you kill him?'

'What difference does it make?'

'I'd like to be sure he's dead.'

'Why?'

She pursed her lips. 'It was not only on your side of the border that he…hurt…women.'

This time, Cate did not hesitate. Her hand gripped Stella's. 'You?'

She shook her head, thankful. Her parents had made sure of that. But Storwick lands were wide and not everyone was so careful. 'But no one mourns his death.' She gripped Cate's hand in return. 'He *is* dead, isn't he?'

Cate withdrew her hand, crossed her arms and nodded.

'Then where's his body?'

Cate nodded towards the hill. 'Up there. At the bottom of a ravine. Where it belongs.'

'And you killed him?' Somehow, it seemed important for a woman to take her revenge.

Something shifted behind Cate's eyes. 'If I told you the whole story, you wouldn't believe it.'

She opened her lips to say she would, but the woman's eyes were hard again. 'Let us begin again. My name is Stella,' she said, instead.

Cate nodded. 'Cate Gilnock, wife of Johnnie Brunson.' When she spoke his name, Stella saw the first softness the woman had shown.

Aye, this clan was a hard one. But they were both woman, after all, perhaps with more in common than they knew. Maybe, just maybe, Cate would help persuade Rob to let her see her father.

'Do you know,' she began, hopeful, 'where they are holding Hobbes Storwick?'

Cate parted her lips and Stella held her breath. 'Did Rob not tell you?'

Should she lie? No. She'd be too easily discovered. She shook her head.

But the Warrior Woman was Brunson before all. 'Then neither will I.' She turned for the door.

'Please—'

'I lost my father to Willie Storwick. I cannot forgive that.'

'But my father tried to stop him. Punished him. Banned him from the family. And I want to see my father, before...'

Before he is as dead as yours.

Stella held her breath, suddenly realising what she had done.

Too late to hide her parentage now.

And all for naught, for Cate was shaking her head. 'I will tell you this. Rob sent word to your family that you are here.'

'Thank you for telling me.' Relief. The ransom must be on the way. Rob Brunson would no doubt be glad to wash his hands of her. 'When will I be going home?'

Cate looked away. 'Rob will have to tell you.'

The door closed and Stella sank on to the stool. Soon. Soon she would be away from every one of the Brunsons.

Johnnie returned with the news that Carwell had sent word of Stella Storwick's capture to the English warden.

'And?' Rob asked.

Johnnie shook his head. 'Nothing. The English warden said he informed them, but there was no demand we release her. No offer of ransom. Not even a threat to attack.'

Rob turned it over in his mind. More than strange. No Borderer worth his salt would let such an affront lie.

'All they said was that "in consideration of who she was, they hoped we would treat her kindly."'

'Who she is? She's a Storwick. I've treated her more kindly than she deserved.' He tried to puzzle it out. 'The message sounds the same as the one they sent when we told them we held Hobbes. Did they say nothing more of him?'

Johnnie shook his head. 'What's worse,' he added, 'is that the man cannot rise from his bed.'

'A wound?' Rob tried to remember the battle.

His brother shook his head.

'Then what ails him?'

Johnnie shrugged. They knew naught of medicine and Aberdeen was far away. 'Thomas and Bessie have tried to make him comfortable, but...'

Cruel of his kin, to leave him in the care of the enemy. 'Who leads them now?' A new man? An untried son afraid to act?

'Thomas isn't sure. Storwick has no sons. Only a daughter.'

Rob shook his head. 'A bad situation.' Without a clear leader, a clan could disintegrate. Infighting, squabbles, no decisions, no one to follow. Bad for the Storwicks if true.

But for the Brunsons? Well, it could be equally so.

He looked at his brother and tried to be sure he heard rightly. 'So the Storwicks do not demand the return of either prisoner?'

'Impossible to believe, but true.'

He had assumed he would be rid of the lass

soon and richer for it. What would he do if they didn't want her? He certainly couldn't just let her go. He knew how to confront, how to fight. He knew how to defend the tower if they came after her. But this…

'Perhaps they plan a raid and think to trick us.' He was relieved to speak his thoughts aloud to his brother. When a head man spoke, he must be certain.

But there was something there. Some reason for the silence. Some reason strong enough to send Stella Storwick across the border.

'Have you told him the important news?' Cate walked in, her smile all at odds with talk of war.

Johnnie caught her hand, his face a mirror of her delight.

Rob felt a moment's pang. What would it be like to share a smile with someone who knew your thoughts without words?

He'd never know.

Cate's smile expanded. 'Bessie's to be a mother.'

'And Thomas a father,' Johnnie said, smiling at her.

Rob struggled to smile, but it felt as if his sister had betrayed him. Or that he had failed. Neither he nor Johnnie had fathered a Brunson babe. Now, the youngest of them all would be the first to spawn the next generation. 'When?'

'In the autumn, she thinks.' Cate was the one to answer. Johnnie deferred to her, silent, as if everything to do with birthing was women's work.

Rob caught Johnnie's eye. No Brunson woman had ever died giving birth, and yet…

'I'll be with her,' Cate said, as if she had heard his thoughts. She did not ask permission.

He nodded, as if he were giving it anyway. Then he closed the door on his thoughts. The Storwicks, including Stella, were his immediate problem.

'How does the Storwick lass?' Johnnie asked.

The delight on Cate's face died. 'Living like royalty, I'd say.' She looked at Rob, as if the fault were his.

It was. Treat her kindly indeed. He had treated her too kindly.

'And where do *we* sleep tonight?' Cate added.

When they were at the tower, John and Cate shared Bessie's old room. The one he had kindly given to Stella Storwick.

'Take mine,' he said. 'I'll not be sleeping much tonight.' He rose. 'We ride tomorrow.'

Johnnie looked to Cate and then back at Rob. 'Where?'

His smile was grim. 'Let's just say I've a taste for fish.'

'So now you're going fishing so Hobbes Storwick's daughter can feast on salmon?'

Stella. In consideration of who she was... *Hobbes Storwick, who had no sons, but only a daughter.*

Only a daughter...

A daughter who must have laughed at him for being more simple than Wat Gregor.

But a daughter who, for some reason, they would leave with him.

He rose and left the room without a word.

A fist bludgeoned Stella's door and she rose, but Rob did not wait for permission to enter.

'They know you're here.'

'My family?' A smile burst forth. No matter who knew her family now. 'When do I go home?'

He said nothing, but stared at her face, as if searching for a secret message.

She tried again. 'When will I be ransomed?'

His black expression shifted, slightly, and she thought she saw a sneer. And then, just for a moment, perhaps it was pity.

'It seems you are not so special after all,' he said.

A chill, though the air was cool. 'What do you mean?'

'I mean no one wants to pay a penny for you.'

'That can't be.' Although she knew it could. Her mother might argue, but Humphrey and Oswyn were locked in an irreconcilable battle. What one wanted, the other opposed, and neither was strong enough now to sway the rest of the family to his side.

She looked at Rob again and forced herself to assume a disdainful expression. There had to be another explanation.

'Or if it is,' she continued, 'it's because they won't pay your blackmail. They'll come and get me instead.'

'Will they now? Then why haven't they come after Hobbes Storwick in all these months?'

Because they were hoping he would die first.

The words seared themselves into her brain, coming so quick and sure that she knew, finally, they were true. Yes, she and her mother had mourned and fretted at her father's absence. Her cousins had not. Mayhap that was why they had delayed and dithered so long in the first place. All they had to do was wait. The black bile would kill him and they'd be left to deal only with each other.

And how special will you be then? something whispered.

There would be no special place for Stella when they took over. What could she do then? Join a convent and mutter perpetual prayers? That was not the life she wanted. She wanted what ordinary people had. Children.

A husband.

'They haven't come for him because they are abiding by the laws of the borders, unlike you godforsaken Brunsons.' She could let him think nothing else.

'They did express concern for your safety.'

'They said nothing of…nothing more?' She had kept her secret from the Brunsons, and for a few days, she had enjoyed the anonymity she craved. No one had stared at her, as if at any moment she would wave her hand and multiply the loaves and fishes.

But no one had given her privileges, either.

'They did express concern for your safety,' he repeated, 'and asked that I treat you kindly, in consideration of who you are.' He leaned forwards, looming over her, cutting off escape just as surely as he had that first day in the hills. With each step, she had to move back, until the bed pressed against her legs and the mattress gave way behind her.

He took a deep breath, and she felt herself struggle for air. 'Who *are* you, Stella Storwick?'

She matched him, now, standing as tall as she could, though that brought her head only as high as his chin. For the last few days, she had been ignored, even disrespected as never in her life.

She took a deep breath. She had suffered his food, his insults and his disdain. It was past time he realised who she was. 'I'm Hobbes Storwick's only child.'

His expression did not alter. 'Aye.'

'That's all you have to say?' She had expected…something more.

'You tell me nothing I don't know.'

Aye, a moment's confession to Cate had overcome her careful omission. 'And still you treat me this way?'

'What way is that, pretty Stella? What did you expect?'

Ah, that was the question of her life. What did her parents expect of her? What miracle was God waiting for her to perform? 'Respect.'

'Respect? I've given you a room and food and when you insisted on floundering in Liddel Water like a trout on a line, I let you do that, too. I've given you near the treatment I'd offer an honoured guest. What more do you want?'

How could she explain? She didn't even know. But at home, she was special. Here, she was…

She turned her back on him. She couldn't think when his breath brushed against her cheek.

From behind her, he leaned against the mattress, trapping her, his arms as unyielding as if she had been behind the bars of an iron yett. 'What would have happened to me,' he began, 'if I'd been the one captured wandering alone too close to Storwick land?'

His hands moved to cup her shoulders. His breath burned her ear. She could not think, yet she did not feel fear, but connection. One she didn't want.

She turned, breaking his hold. 'With honour.'

'Honour? This from a family of one of the most dishonourable rogues who ever drew breath on either side of the border! From a family that violated the very sanctity of Truce Day? Don't speak of honour to me, Stella Storwick.'

'My father disowned Willie.' Such a cut was unheard of, but sometimes, she wondered whether he should have done more. After what the man had done…

'Strange to disown a man and then put us to the torch to avenge his death.'

'That is honour, is it not? The standing up for family, even when they are wrong?'

She could see by the look in his eyes she had given him pause.

But it no longer mattered. None of that mattered. 'So you know who I am and it seems I will not be going back to my family soon.' She turned away, hunching in on herself. 'Could I see him? Would you take me to where he is?'

'Why?'

She turned back, no longer able to hide the tears. 'Because...' she swallowed '...he is dying.'

Chapter Six

The pain on her face hit him like a blow.

Bad enough to die in your bed, as his father had. Worse to die in an enemy's.

No man should leave his kin to that fate.

Not rising from his bed Johnnie had said. And she knew. Or was it a trick? Did she lie? 'What is his sickness?'

She kept her arms crossed, as if trying to hold something inside. 'The wasting disease. He's… It started near Yuletide.'

So he was not well enough to go to Truce Day. Instead, he was home when they had attacked, but not well enough to command. Storwick was a worthy opponent. If he had been at his best, the triumph would never have been won so easily. But Rob had little time to ponder the man's health. He only assumed the old warrior had been injured.

'Tell me where he is. Pity me at least that much.'

He did pity her. And he didn't want to.

Rob still mourned the fact that there had been no farewell. One night, they went to bed. The next morning, his father didn't wake.

Her eyes were on him, expectant.

Rob sighed. 'He's at Carwell Castle.'

She swallowed and turned away, covering her lips with her hand. Aye, she knew what that meant. Rescue would be near impossible, even if her kin tried. But for some reason, her kin wanted neither Hobbes nor Stella Storwick to come home.

She turned to face him, arrogant chin and proud eyes firmly in place again. 'You want me here no more than I want to be here. If they aren't going to come for either of us, what is the harm of letting me go to him?'

Did she move closer? Or did he?

Her hands touched his chest. She raised her eyes to his. His hands cupped her cheeks and tilted her head, bringing the soft curve of her lower lip close enough to touch his…

Sunlight. Shadow. Thunder. What shook him had no word. No thought. An urge as elemental as battle. But much more dangerous.

Her body pressed against his and his lips pressed against hers, but more gently now. No, not the desire to conquer. The urge to connect, to join…

Their lips parted. She sighed.

The sound restored his senses. He opened his eyes and pulled himself away.

Weak. Weak to be lured by a woman into giving in to her wishes. If he allowed this, she would ask for something else. That might even be part of the plan. If he took her west, beyond the protection of the tower, his men would be open to attack.

But she still stood there, eyes closed, a slight smile on her face, and it took all his strength to speak.

'No.'

Her eyes fluttered open and he saw her return to reality with a jolt as painful as his. Hate rushed into her narrowed eyes, killing the soft-ness. 'You are a cruel man, Black Rob Brunson.'

'I'm a head man. You should understand what that means.' He turned to leave, hoping to break the spell of her eyes.

'What happens to me now?'

He wished he could say, but he closed his mind to her question, for he did not know. What kind of family wouldn't come for its own?

He only knew he did not want her to leave.

He had been too lenient with the woman, Rob decided, the next morning. And now that she knew there would be no ransom, she might try to escape, so he told the guard to let her wander the buildings with Wat, but not to let her leave the courtyard, even to check for fish.

Instead, he took Johnnie down to the stream to check the newly built weir.

It held nary a fin.

His brother was looked from Rob to the dam of sticks and raised an eyebrow.

Rob sighed. 'Say your piece. You've been hold-ing your tongue all morning.'

'It's illegal to build one of these without the King's permission,' Johnnie began.

Rob let out a bitter laugh. 'Let the King add this to my list of sins. It won't be the one he hangs me for.' He had told Stella he would destroy the Storwicks' dam. Now was the time. 'Come. I've a plan. When next we check this trap, it will be full of fish.'

Rob took Johnnie and three men with him. Cate had insisted on joining them, saying she could not abide sharing the air with a Storwick.

'When did you develop a taste for salmon?' Johnnie asked, after they rode west, following Liddel Water through the valley. Beyond Kershopefoote, the burn formed the boundary between Scotland and England and bordered Storwick land.

That's where they would have built the weir.

'I like it well enough,' he said, ignoring the fact that he was riding a raid because his captive had a taste for fish. 'Food hasn't been the same since Bessie left.'

John nodded, silent. No argument with that.

It was his duty to feed his people.

Duty. Responsibility. Battle. Those were what

he knew. If ever peace came, what could he offer those who looked to him then? His father had taught him the hills, the trails, horses and spears and latch arrows. His father had made him more comfortable on a horse than before the fire.

More comfortable in battle than with a woman.

Once, when he was young and his blood ran hot, he had been tempted by a lass. By more than one, if truth be told. He knew no better then, spilling his seed into stable straw, kissing one, two, three women who kissed him back. He never thought to ask why until his father caught him one day and taught him his responsibilities with a leather strap.

'You've no more sense than a sheep.'

He stood straight, ignoring the pain, ready to take his punishment, if only he knew what it was for. 'There's plenty of bastard brothers reiving the Borders,' he said. Plenty of men and women loving where they would. The English remarked on it.

'Aye. And those girls would love there to be plenty more. Do you think they lie with you only because of your good looks? They want to claim they carry the babe of the son of the head man.'

So then he knew. He had not earned a woman. Not for *who* he was. Only for *what* he was. The son of the head man. That was all he was and all he could offer.

If he was not that man, he was nothing at all.

So he became suspicious of women, though many looked at him with smiles in their eyes. Did they smile at him? Or at the head man?

Well, he knew the answer for this woman. Stella Storwick cared nothing for Rob Brunson. It was the head man of the Brunsons she hated and if he could accept the smiles, he must take the curses. That, too, was his duty.

The memories followed him for near ten miles, as they rode close to the water. Some places, they could ride beside the stream. In others, the bank was too narrow and uncertain, so they veered away, peering through the spring green leaves, coming thick on the trees.

Early in the afternoon, Rob held up a hand to halt the horses, listening. A horse stomped damp ground and swished his tail. The wind rustled live leaves and dead. And something in the sound of the water had changed.

He motioned them to dismount and they crept

towards the stream, alert for anything other than birds and squirrels. Staying in the shelter of the trees, he looked at the water. The river made a sharp turn here and narrowed. And there, stretching from the English side, was a construction very similar to the one he'd built.

But in this one, fish scales flashed, shining like sunlight underwater.

He smiled.

When Rob rode into the courtyard, Stella was the first thing he laid eyes on. She had Wat next to her, nestled on a bench in the last corner of sunshine, and she seemed to be trying to teach him to count on his fingers.

Foolish waste.

Swinging off the horse, he grabbed the sack of precious wriggling silver and walked over to her. 'Here's fish for you,' he said, dropping the overflowing bag in her lap. Some of them flopped and wiggled, as if they had a little life left. 'May you choke on them.'

Wat laughed and bent to pick up the ones that had fallen out of the bag and into the dirt.

With the bag of smelly fish on her lap, Stella

could not rise, but her eyes flashed at him and he thought she would reach for one and slap his face with it.

'Take the bag to Beggy, Wat,' she said, still looking at Rob. Then she scooped the fish back in and guided the boy's fingers tightly around the opening. 'Can you carry it?'

He nodded, proud, and dragged it across the dirt to the kitchen.

Stella stood. 'So we'll be eating Storwick fish tonight?'

'They had no names on them.' He had, somehow, expected her to be pleased. Instead, he faced the same angry woman he had left. 'We'll have fish in our own trap soon. Worthy of a Brunson.'

'What makes a Brunson so worthy?'

Her very question a challenge he'd never had to answer. '*I'm* a Brunson.' He knew what that meant. He was rugged and strong and steadfast as the First Brunson, whose tale was told in the ballad. The man who had been left for dead by his enemies, deserted by his friends. The man who was loyal to this land and his people above all. That's what Rob Brunson was. That was what any Brunson must be.

She tilted her head, as if ignorant of all the name entailed. 'And I'm Stella Storwick,' she answered.

Not just a Storwick, an individual. Well, if he were a Storwick, he would separate himself from the rest, too. 'And who are the Storwicks but a bunch of savage killers?'

'And what are the Brunsons but the same?'

'Brunsons have been here longer than the kings. We're descended from a Viking.'

'Yes. I've heard of your precious brown-eyed Viking.' She rolled her eyes.

Nothing he said could impress this woman. 'He was more than that. He and his men came from far across the sea.'

'No women?'

He shrugged. What was there to say of women? He had never been easy with them. 'These were warriors. They fought their way up to this valley before one of their own betrayed them and they were slain, almost every one. And the rest left him for dead.' Deserted him. Bastards.

Not family. Family wouldn't desert you.

'But he was not?'

'He was too stubborn to die. Even the enemy left him for dead. But when he woke, recovered enough to walk, he staggered away, hoping to find his people.'

She raised her brows, showing no proper respect for his story. 'Near death, alone, unarmed, he rises like Lazarus and walks away?'

'Aye. Exactly.' He had never questioned the truth of it. 'And he vowed he would never leave this valley. That's the will that makes a Brunson.' He carried that strength in his blood. 'Can the Storwicks top that?'

Something flickered in her eyes, like sunlight under water.

Chapter Seven

No, she wanted to say. *But I can.*

But her story was the one she wanted to escape. Here, finally, she could.

'Well,' he asked again, 'have the Storwicks no stories?'

'Of course we have stories.' Every family had stories.

'What kind?'

His question took her back. When she was a child, her mother would tell her tales of brave heroes and heroines as if handing her a platter of sweetcakes, waiting for her to pick one. As if she could somehow discover in those tales the reason she had been saved.

There were stories of men who rode on quests or laid in wait to ambush raiders and save the

Storwick lands, but her favourite tale was none of those.

It was the story of the Lost Storwick.

Her mother had not learned that one from the monks.

'The story is told,' she began, 'of a Storwick woman long ago.'

'A woman?'

Damn his look of shock. 'Yes. A woman.' She paused, waiting for him to subdue his surprise.

He nodded and she went on.

'Long ago, perhaps in the time your Vikings came to this valley, this woman's husband cast her aside, for he believed she was a doer of magic who had caused the son of his first wife to fall ill and die.'

'Wasn't he afraid she would work her magic on him as well?

She frowned to be interrupted. The tale must be told a certain way. 'There was never any proof, nor any accusations that she had worked ill on anyone else.' Some thought he had invented the story because he was tired of her, but Rob Brunson thought little enough of her family as it was. 'Still, his son had fallen ill and died and he wished for someone to blame.'

'And the family allowed it? Or had she committed a sin?'

She put her hands on her hips. 'Did I interrupt your tale? Would I grab your tongue if you were singing the Ballad of the Brunsons?'

The muscles in his cheek moved, as if he had clamped his teeth against future words.

'So, this woman withdrew to a hut on the settlement's edge and barred the door. Her family brought her food and left it outside, where she could reach it from the window, but for many days, they would bring fresh food and find she had not touched what they brought the day before.'

His expression was angry still, but she thought she glimpsed a touch of sadness, too.

'Finally, one day, after her family had seen their pile of offerings grew untouched for a week, they pounded the door, trying to get in. She must have heaped rocks against it from the inside, for they pushed and shoved and the door would barely budge.

'And then they pounded on the shutters that shielded the window, but still they could not break in and they heard no sound from within.'

Rob leaned closer and seemed to be holding his breath. 'Then what?'

She held back a smile. 'When they finally pushed through, the hut was empty.'

'Empty? Where was she?'

'No one ever really knew. Some said God had snatched her and sent her right to Heaven. Some said she had run away and made a new home for herself on the other side of the fells, where no one knew who she was. But they never found a body, neither in the hut nor in the hills.

'And some claim her ghost still haunts the hills, looking for home.'

Stella liked the story because she understood that woman. She was not cast aside, no, but she was set apart. Stared at. Held at arm's length. As if everyone was waiting for her to do... something. Finally, like the Lost Storwick, she wanted to disappear from the burden that had been placed on her. Was God going to snatch her, too, from the earth some day? If so, she was ready.

* * *

Something in the wistfulness of her face touched him. He fought it. He cared nothing for Storwick legends and lore. He wanted only to know who they were today and how they might threaten his family.

'Who runs your family now?'

Her eyes cleared and she looked at him again, as if she were coming back from wandering in those hills like the Lost Storwick. 'Who?'

'Yes, who?' He should not have asked so bluntly. She was probably wise enough to realise that the information alone was valuable. More so if he tried to bludgeon her with words.

'My cousins.'

Two words after a long pause. The first hint of who was in charge of the Storwicks and why they had been so quiet.

Cousins. No single leader. No successor, named or natural. That meant quarrels. And that explained much of what he had seen, or not seen, from across the border since they stole Hobbes Storwick away.

For some reason, that angered him. 'Yet they do not demand your return.' He held the daughter of their head man and they could bestir themselves to do no more than plead that he treat her kindly. 'Are they not men?'

'Of course they are men. We may have legends of women, but women do not rule our family any more than they do yours.'

That was not what he meant, of course. He meant they were not the men they should have been. The kind of man his father had raised him to be.

Wat returned from the kitchen, ending the conversation, but he thought, as he left her, that she might be wrong. Brunson women held a wider sway than many he'd seen.

Marriage. The idea came to him of a sudden. Yet he was no good with women. Nor they with him.

His father had been right, all those years ago. He was head man. That's all he was. No one would ever love him for himself.

The King's notice arrived the next week. King James would be coming to the Borders himself in June to see that justice was done and to punish the guilty.

Rob stared at it after Johnnie read it to him. Then they looked at each other, silent for a moment.

He had known this day would come. Known it every step of the way he had chosen. And chose it anyway.

'He'll have a list to choose from when he brings justice for the Brunsons.' There was some pride in saying it.

'Aye,' Johnnie said, trying to smile. 'No doubt the herald chapped his lips putting us to the horn.'

Three blasts to announce a man as rebel, traitor, outlaw to all of Edinburgh. Aye, the horn would sound long and loud.

The King named each of them for a different reason. First, he had sent Johnnie home to bring the Brunson men to fight at the King's side. They sent none.

Then, Rob refused to swear the King's Great Oath against his enemies. And when the English Storwick swine disappeared, well, he blamed the Brunsons for that, too.

Worst of all, for love of Bessie Brunson, the Scottish Warden refused to bring in the Brunsons and instead of holding the Truce Day promised by treaty, rode with them across the border to pluck Hobbes Storwick from his home.

Aye, even Carwell, at the end, had defied the King for love of a Brunson.

Johnnie looked at the message again, smile gone. 'He'll come. And he'll bring an army with him.' Into their valley. 'And then he'll find out we're holding the Storwick wench—'

Rob shook his head. He did not need to hear the rest. By the end, the Brunsons would be dangling from the trees above a valley burned to ash. Whether they held the Storwick woman or not, he doubted that would change.

Side by side, the brothers pondered, silent.

'He might not kill us,' Johnnie said, finally. 'Maybe he'll hold you, warded, for our good behaviour.'

Rob shook his head. 'He tried that with Bessie.' For all the good it did. He would know now there was no use in that.

'He'll come for Carwell, too.'

Carwell, Scottish Warden, King's man, who had been tasked with bringing a hostage to the

King and fell in love with that hostage, Bessie Brunson, instead.

'Rob, you need to forgive her, forgive both of them. The King thinks—'

'The King may think Carwell is a Brunson.' And he had already charged Thomas Carwell to arrest them and bring them in. Carwell had refused. One thing the man had done right, Rob was forced to admit, grudgingly. 'I don't.'

'We could disappear. Ride into the hills and the King would never be able to find us. He'll get tired. He'll go home—'

'I won't run. Not from anyone.'

'Well, then,' John said, 'I guess that means King James will be in for a fight.'

Rob looked at him. 'You're the one who said we should reconcile with the King.'

'I reconciled with you instead.' His quick grin disappeared and he put a hand on Rob's shoulder 'We've some time. Maybe there will be another way.'

Johnnie at his side. Family. A comfort. All.

I want to see my father.

Aye. Family meant something to Stella Storwick, too. Should he take her to her father, then?

Before the King came, certainly, if he were to do it. Would she even thank him if he did? No, she'd think it no more than her due.

She was different from what he expected. Certainly different from Bessie, who had always worked silently in the background.

He looked at Johnnie, wanting to ask what it was like, to have a woman. Of course, he'd seen the way Johnnie looked at Cate. The way he had protected her, but of course, any man would do that for his family. But this was more.

Different.

And Carwell had done the same for Bessie, he had to admit. Protected her even when it put his own position at risk.

If he had a good strong woman at his left hand, well, that might make everything easier. But perhaps it was just as well. A head man must think of all his clan, not just his woman.

And he must certainly not think of a Storwick woman.

Yet later, Rob found himself standing outside her room, leaning against the stone wall, hitting it with his fists. He did not know what to do with this woman, nor with the feelings and doubts she raised.

Suddenly, he looked down and there was Wat, staring up at him admiringly. Ah, the little lad, looking like a cherub. Looking at him as if he expected…what?

He and Wat studied each other for a moment, silent. Then, Wat turned his back, went to the door of Stella's room and knocked.

Stella opened it, looking down as if she had known from the height of the knock who would be there.

'Gudein, Stella. Time to play?'

Ah, this was the monster he had unleashed. Telling her she could look after the boy.

She crouched down so she could speak directly to the boy, not sparing Rob a glance. 'What would you like to do today, Wat?'

'Fish!' he said with a squeal.

She glanced up at Rob. 'If the laird will let us leave the walls.'

'Did you not get your fill of fish last week?' Yet the Storwick fish had been long eaten.

Her damned green eyes accused him, though her lips smiled. She knew exactly what she had said. If he refused the child here and now, the boy would think him nothing but cruel.

Hell. Let her run back across the border if she must. Then he'd be rid of her.

'Go.' He started down the stairs, but looked back to see Stella and Wat hugging. 'I'll expect fish to eat tonight!'

And their obvious affection made him feel even more alone.

Rob was both relieved and chagrined to see fish on his plate that evening.

She spoke not a word about it, but seemed to smile with every bite. Waiting. Waiting, dammit, for him to admit she had done it. That the special princess and her halfwit had managed to put Brunson fish on the table.

Well, he spoke none of it either until he had finished the last bite and fed his pride, as well as his stomach. Black Rob Brunson was a proud man, and a stubborn one, but the woman deserved her due.

Little Wat had spent the meal spinning in happiness, tugging at the men's tunics, begging them to smile. And they did, many of them. Those that had not given him a glance before. Those who had dismissed an idiot boy.

Those like Rob.

But even he smiled to see the child so happy.

He pushed the plate away. She lifted her brows, waiting.

'The fish filled the stomach.'

'I helped Beggy. Cooked as well as caught it.'

Grudgingly, he said more. 'Tasty.'

For the first time, she looked abashed. 'Thank you. I wasn't really sure I could do it.'

He wished she had not said it. It made her human, somehow. He did not want to think of her as human. It was easier when he just thought of her as 'Storwick.' Or as a dragon.

'The weir was filled with fish aplenty.'

'We'll eat well, then.'

'As long as...'

'As long as the Storwicks don't rebuild?'

She shook her head. 'My cousins can't agree on whether the sun will rise.' She bit her lip, realising she had said too much.

'They can't what?' Quarrels, then. More than he'd suspected.

She shook her head. 'I can't remember.'

He was not a subtle man. What he wanted to know, he asked. *Who heads the clan now? What kind of men are they? Why have they not acted?*

But she knew what she had said. And now she would say no more, particularly if he tried a frontal assault. Sometimes, in a raid, it was better to ride the longer way around and come from the unexpected angle.

He pushed the empty platter aside and rose. Wat's mother collected him for bed and Beggy took the dishes away.

'Would you walk with me, then?'

'I should help Beggy.'

He motioned one of the other girls, who scurried to carry dishes. 'She'll have help. I've...' He hated to say he had rearranged the household because of her. And it wasn't true. Not exactly. 'Come.'

Daylight lingered longer now and they wandered up to the top of the tower. He looked over his valley with the same satisfaction he always felt. The clouds were tinged with pink and he strained his eyes, wondering whether he could pick out some of the sheep at the edge of the hills.

Danger could still lurk there, over the border, but tonight, with a woman beside him, he could almost believe in a peaceful life that included a wife who loved *him* and not just the head man.

Maybe even a son…

She leaned on the edge of the wall, gazing south. Was she looking towards her home? Was she wondering why they would not come for her?

'I hear,' she said, her very voice signalling a new topic, 'that you are a singing man.'

He shrugged. 'Aye.'

'And that you are the only one who knows all the verses of the Ballad of the Brunsons.'

'Bessie does, as well.'

But Bessie no longer lived here. Who would sing the song when he was gone? Who was there for him to teach, as his father had taught him?

She looked up at him. 'It is beautiful. I can see why you love it so.'

He opened his mouth to argue, but instead, he fell into her eyes, as green as the grass would be at midsummer. The cheekbones that had seemed too sharp now sculpted her face into a perfect shape.

He turned away, but he could feel her, beside

him, close enough that he could put an arm around her. Too close. Too tempting. Aye, it had been too long since he'd kissed a woman.

He looked up and saw the first star of evening. Looked away, not wanting to be reminded of her, but she was beside him, she was everywhere…

He stopped thinking and took her lips.

And in that moment, it felt strong and hard and right and there was nothing beyond man and woman.

Yet her lips did not yield. They coaxed him further, deeper. Some buried part of his brain wondered how many she had kissed before. Some unburied part wanted to make sure she'd remember his.

He was not a cruel man, but he was a strong one, accustomed to action and battle, striking first and talking later. Her lips made him want to linger. Her mouth opened to him, her tongue tasted his mouth, he tasted hers, and then he forgot who she was, and who he was, and he did not try to remember.

Stella let herself be held, be taken, be swept into his arms to forget everything. No place, no

time, no Storwick or Brunson. Not even separate people...

She didn't know what brought her back to the
truth. That she was being held by a man who
was her mortal enemy. She must have stiffened.
He nearly dropped her. She nearly fell.

She stumbled. Stepped back. Touched her lips
and looked up at him.

And there was nothing but breath and the
sound of her heart pounding in her ears and the
heat that had begun with her lips and curled its
way down to flicker like fire deep within her.

Then there were footsteps at the end of the
wall.

He stepped between her and the sound, as if
by hiding her, all they had done would disappear. It was one of the men, guarding the tower,
looking out over the land. She did not raise her
eyes to see which one. Nor to see if he had seen
her.

Rob's hand circled her arm and they left the
parapet, both still breathing as if they had run a
long, long way. Somehow, something more than
his body seemed to surround her. Even where

he did not touch her, even though they did not look at each other, they moved as one.

He near threw her into the room, as if by letting go, by putting distance between them, he could break it off, could rip the feelings apart.

His chest rose and fell. And the hardness of his jaw clenched… 'Ye'll not get me to take you to your father that way. So don't try it again.'

The door closed.

Her knees gave way and she sank on to the bed. Then, she clenched her fist, as strong and tight as a warrior's, and pounded the mattress in fury. Whether her fury was for him or herself she wasn't sure.

If only that *had* been why. If only she had kissed him with calculation, hoping to spin his head, to make him let her go to see her father, to go home, to go anywhere. None of that had crossed her mind. It had been only him.

Him. Him. Him.

Each word pounded into the mattress with her fist.

When had she last been kissed? She could not remember. Once, perhaps. Twice. But always with respect. As if she were some sort of glass

treasure. Not like this. Not in a way that unleashed a wild beast inside her.

Oh, she knew women enjoyed it, but she had
never felt this…hunger. As if she wanted at once
to devour and be devoured.

It was wrong. All of it. For her to even touch
such a man, touch the enemy like that.

No doubt he was the calculating one. He must
have wanted simply to confuse her. But still,
still…

Rob spoke less than usual the next day. His
lips were numb, as if he had drunk too much
ale, and every time he moved them, he feared
they would shout aloud that he had kissed her.

It would not happen again. She had lured him
in and turned his head around. He had been too
much with her, spent more hours in her company
than with anyone but his family.

Time to think of the future. A head man should
marry. He needed someone to run the castle.
Someone to bear his children.

Someone not afraid to sit next to him at meals.

A headman needed a wife. Someone appropriate. Someone who would keep his mind far away from Stella Storwick.

If that were possible.

Chapter Eight

Rob rode with Johnnie the next day, waiting for the right time to speak of marriage. He had to talk to someone about how to find a bride. And there was no one else.

'Sheep will be moving into the hills soon,' Johnnie said, casting his eyes to those hills, looking, always, for riders. 'Maybe it would be better to have the men shift them to new places.'

There was Johnnie again. Always trying to change things. The man, the sheep, the dog, and the patch of ground were wedded. 'Herder and his sheep know their place. To pull them away will put them all off their feed.'

Johnnie sighed. And pushed no more.

It was noontime when they stopped in the hills for a bwannock.

'I've been thinking,' Rob began.

Johnnie waited a moment. Rob waited for him to ask.

'About what?' Johnnie said, finally.

'That it is time for me to wed.'

Johnnie had been at court and that training must have been what kept him from spitting his oatcake across the grass. 'Have you now?'

'Head man. Should have a wife.'

'Well, I highly recommend it.' Johnnie's tone was more restrained than he had expected. 'May you be as happy as Cate and I.'

Rob gave a grunt. Happy was not the point.

Johnnie waited for him to speak. He did not.

'You've found someone, then?' Johnnie said, finally.

He cleared his throat, but it sounded like a growl. 'I thought you could help.'

There was a grin. Johnnie was near laughing at him. 'Usually, falling in love is something a man needs no help with.'

'It's not love I want!' Love meant someone else could control him. 'It's a wife!'

'Well, you can't have mine,' his brother retorted.

'Johnnie, you are not the head man.' Johnnie

was the younger son. He could marry for love if he liked. 'I need a wife the clan will accept. Respect. One who can manage things.'

His mother had ridden their lands to visit all the families. She and Bessie both had known how to feed an army with a pound of mutton. That was the kind of woman he needed.

Not someone who would spread flour all over the kitchen.

'I thought…' He cleared his throat. 'I thought you could help me find someone…fitting.'

Johnnie was silent for a while, glancing at Rob as if he'd grown an extra head.

'Well?' he said, finally.

Johnnie eyed him, not like a brother. 'This could be a path to reconcile with the King. Select a woman he'd approve of. Ask his permission—'

'I don't care whether the King approves.'

'Then why do you care who's appropriate? Just find someone you love.'

Because no one I love will ever love me.

'Can't you just once do as I ask?' It came out as a yell.

He just needed to direct his seed at someone

other than Stella Storwick. Fortunately, Johnnie would never suspect *that* weakness.

Johnnie stared at him. 'Aye, then. I'll think on who would be a match for you.'

Rob nodded, but did not say thank you.

Stella had not expected Cate Gilnock to seek her out again. They had a truce, you might say. Enough so that the woman would not kill her in her sleep.

At least, she hoped not.

But the next day, as she and Wat played by the stream, here came the woman and her huge beast of a dog. They stopped when they saw her and the dog came up to sniff her up and down and in some very private places.

So that was the hound, she thought, standing rigid as he sniffed her. The one who, if the whispers she heard were right, had tracked Willie Storwick to his death.

She patted his head. *Good dog.*

'His name is Belde,' Cate said.

Stella nodded and the dog moved on to sniff Wat, but the dog knew him and they ran off to play together, leaving the two women to talk.

Cate eyed her steadily. Stella lifted her head. She was not going to be cowed by this woman who dressed as a man.

'They tell me,' Cate began, looking at her with a wary eye, 'that you are no better cook than I.'

Criticism. But yet, aye. Cate's no cook, Beggy had said. Something else they had in common.

She shook her head. 'Beggy won't let me into the kitchen unless I'm bringing fresh fish.' That, at least, she did not mangle. 'It's not home.' More than she ought to reveal.

'Are you all right, then?'

Stella blinked. Concern was not what she had expected. A rush of tears nearly spilled over. She bit her lip. 'Well enough.' She would not be lulled. 'Rob Brunson is a bit of a brute.'

Cate shook her head and smiled. 'But he's not hurt you.'

It was not a question.

She had to smile back. 'Nay. But he yells.'

'When he speaks at all.'

They both laughed, then. But after, there was only silence and Wat's squeals and the gurgle of the water.

'I saw him,' Cate said, at last. 'Your father.'

Stella's heart dropped to her stomach and she reached out to squeeze Cate's hand. None of the rest mattered now. 'Tell me.'

Cate glanced up at her eyes, then lowered hers. A sign the news was bad. 'He's not well.'

Now she gripped, hard. 'They've not hurt him, have they?'

Now Cate's eyes were the ones angered. 'He's a sick man. You knew that. Don't go accusing the Brunsons. Thomas and Bessie have done more for him than any Storwick would do for us.'

She struggled against tears. Somehow, she knew Cate was right. 'He's dying, isn't he?'

'I'm no physic—'

Stella let go of her hand and turned away, shaking her head. 'I know. That was why I came.' Running across the border with no more plan than a child, frightened without her father. 'I wanted to see him, to bring him home to die. And Rob wouldn't even tell me where he is. He won't let me go...'

She turned back, holding Cate's brown eyes now. Maybe this woman, even though...

'Would you...?'

The words trailed off. Only dumb hope remained.

But while sympathy lurked in Cate's gaze, there had been too much pain before. She shook her head. 'You ask me to forgive too much.'

Again, this life seemed to throw back to her all the ills her family had done. But hers had not been the only one. 'Do you think we've never been hurt? Brunsons have blood on their hands, too.'

Something shifted in Cate's brown eyes. 'It will never end, will it?'

Stella's shoulders slumped. She looked down at her hands and shook her head.

And she did not look up again until Cate, calling the dog to her side, had gone.

With a wary eye, Rob watched Cate approach. She rarely talked to him alone now that she and Johnnie were well and truly married. He wondered what this was about. Had Johnnie told her he was thinking of marrying? Bah. Couldn't trust your own brother to keep a secret, once he was married.

Well, he needed no goading or advice from Cate on what he should do.

'The Storwick woman,' she began.

He sighed. Not marriage, then. Something worse. 'What of her?'

'We saw her father at Carwell Castle.'

'Aye. That I know.' Unlike Cate to waste breath on unneeded words.

'The man's dying, Rob.'

He steeled his heart. Stella had said the same, right before she begged to go to see him. 'My father died. So did yours. At a Storwick's hand.'

She looked away. 'Aye, and neither you nor I had a chance to say goodbye. But she might. You could give her that chance.'

'Why should she have it if we didn't?'

'Is it the King, then? Are you wondering what he would think?'

'I don't know, or care, what the wee King thinks of anything I do.' That was true, mostly, for good or ill. Johnnie and Thomas would be the ones to confer on that. 'It's my people and my valley I'm sworn to protect.'

And showing a weakness for what a Storwick wanted was not the way to do it.

'Can't you spread peace, instead of misery?'

Womanish question, for all it was Cate who asked him. He had never thought her a weakling. Mayhap marriage had changed her.

Surely not so much that she would take the side of a Storwick against a Brunson. Nothing could change her that much.

But what he could not tell her was how much he wanted to let the woman go. Hell, more than that. He wanted to throw her out of the door.

No. No. And no. That would make him look weak, as if he pandered to her whims. That, he would not allow, no matter who pled the case.

'No. I'll listen to no more about it.'

She must have recognised it as his last word, for she said no more, but her eyes seemed to look at him with pity as she left.

Why? He was doing the right thing. Doing what he must.

Doing what his father would have done.

To Stella's surprise, Cate knocked on her door late in the evening, crossing the threshold before she raised her eyes and spoke. 'I asked him.'

'What?'

'I asked him,' Cate said, again. 'To let you see him.'

She hugged Rob's sister-in-law before logic could stop her. 'Thank you. Thank you.'

Cate shook her head, avoiding Stella's hopeful gaze.

Joy evaporated, leaving pain sharpened by her disappointed hope. 'I should have known he would refuse.'

'He's a stubborn one.'

Aye. She'd never met a man more so. 'But you tried,' she said, swallowing around a lump in her throat. 'That means...thank you. I know that...'

Cate stood silent, waiting.

What had she meant to say? That she knew how terrible her kinsman had been? And how difficult it had been for Cate to help her?

'I'm sorry,' she said, finally. Paltry words for horrid acts, but all she had.

Cate's head jerked in surprise. Then, she nodded. 'You're the only Storwick who ever said so.'

And for a moment, Stella wanted to disown all her kin.

* * *

Rob had said no in no uncertain terms. He was *not* going to let this woman journey to see her father.

Then why did he feel guilty about it? Why did he keep thinking of her when he should have been thinking about the King or the other Storwicks or getting a new bride?

A new bride.

Some unknown, faceless woman who would know how to cook without spilling flour. Who would take the edge off his hunger for a woman.

Who would make no demands.

Instead, he kept looking at Stella Storwick.

She kept looking at him, too. So much that he met her eyes when he had no intention of doing so. Thank goodness she could not see what he was thinking. Of kissing her again.

Of more.

He tried to stay out of her way. Keep her out of his reach, was more like it. He was a man who had not let lust rule him. Not since his father had warned him. But every time he looked at Stella, or thought of Stella, something rumbled and twitched and put him in mind of beds and lips and skin as soft as flower petals.

She continued to spend most of the days with Wat Gregor. Both she and the boy seemed content, doing simple things. He heard both of them laugh. And the boy seemed to have learned something of how to fish and maintain the weir, though she was ever hovering over him.

But one morning, as he sat in the public hall at the edge of the courtyard growling at the account books, he heard again the boy's howling and screaming that had disrupted the tower before she came. He looked out of the window. Wat ran through the courtyard and disappeared from Rob's view.

Then came Stella, running after. Her hair was flying, her cheeks were flushed, and if she had not looked so irritated, he would have thought more about kissing her.

She paused in the middle of the courtyard, looking for the boy. Rob walked out.

'Where is he?' She grabbed Rob's arm. 'Did you see where he went?' No, not irritated. Afraid.

'I heard him right enough.' He pointed to the tower. 'He went that way.' No. He was the one irritated by the feel of her hands on his arm. She had not touched him since... 'Can you not deal with a screaming child?'

He expected her usual air of disdain, but she seemed not even to notice him. 'I hear no screaming now. Something might happen to him.' She looked up now, with pleading eyes he had only seen before when she asked about her father. 'Please. Help me find him.'

'Where does he hide, when you play?'

She shook her head. 'Usually outside. Under a tree where he's not really hidden. Or in the stables.'

'We'll start there.'

Quickly, he saw Wat wasn't there. Rob wasn't worried, not really. Children, he was told, ran away all the time. Maybe it was because she wasn't a mother herself. She obviously had little more experience with children than with cooking, though she was much better with the wee ones.

Still, he felt his anxiety rise with hers.

'Inside the tower, then,' he said, when they had exhausted the courtyard.

When they walked in, she immediately turned to go upstairs.

'Wait,' he said, touching her arm. 'This level first.'

She stiffened and swallowed, as if she had something new to fear.

'Are you sure? He likes the roof. And he might fall off...'

'More places to hide here. Behind barrels, under sacks.'

Nodding, she gripped her fists, as if to summon courage. And he saw the expression flash across her face he had seen that first day when he had threatened to lock her down here.

'Wat?' she called, finally. 'Are you here? Come out, Wat.'

He heard nothing but the scurry of mice feet.

'I'll look up here,' he said, nodding towards the ladder to the entresol, where the barrels were stacked. 'You check the well room.'

He mounted the ladder, quickly.

The lad had been missing too long.

She dragged herself, step by step, to the room in the corner. The iron door was closed. And she released a breath. *He could not have gone in here.*

And she was protected by being kept out.

Still, she clung to the iron bars and peered in. A little light poured in from a small slit in the wall. Enough to let in air, but not enough to allow an arrow to penetrate.

She could see all but one corner. No child in sight. But still… 'Wat?'

He must have been in the hidden corner, for he popped out and screamed, 'Noooooo. Go away. I don't want you.' And started running around the well in the middle of the floor. The well whose cover was slightly askew.

'Wat! Stop it.'

She swung the door open, but something stopped her step. What if she approached and he tripped and…

Before she could think further, Rob was beside her, had gone through the door and scooped Wat into his arms.

Realising who was holding him, the boy immediately stilled. No more kicks or screams. Just the leftover tear on his cheek. But he wrapped his arms around Rob's neck and put his head on his shoulder.

She stepped back and leaned against the wall. Over. And she could breathe again.

'I'll take him.' She held out her arms. Rob had never had patience with the boy, but now, he had an expression more gentle than she had ever seen before.

Seeing her reach for him, Wat turned his head away and squeezed Rob's neck.

She dropped her hands. 'Traitor.'

'What did you do to the boy?' Rob asked.

'I told him he couldn't have an extra bannock.' Such a small treat. Perhaps she should not have been so stern.

The boy's face was still buried in his shoulder, so Rob could afford a grin. Then, he put a stern expression on and a voice to match.

'Listen to me, Wat Gregor.'

The boy lifted his head, slowly, and looked at Rob.

'Are you listening?'

He nodded, enthusiastic.

She stifled a grin of her own.

'From now on,' Rob said, never taking his eyes

from Wat's, 'when this lady says you are to do something, you do as she says. Do you hear me?'

Wat glanced at her, guilty eyes coupled with a pout. He did not nod this time.

'Wat, I'm talking to you.'

'She's an ugly dragon, like you said!'

It took every muscle in her body to hold back the laugh.

Rob, on the other hand, now looked black enough that Wat was cowed. 'Enough. Now tell her you are sorry and you'll not do it again.'

'I'm sorry.' He chewed his words a little more than usual. 'I be good.'

She reached out. 'I'll take him now.'

Her arms brushed Rob's as he handed the boy over. She felt the strength of his arms, felt the rise of his chest and the heat of his breath, and came too close to the strong jaw and the unexpected curve of his lip. No kiss. No touch more than to transfer the boy's vulnerable body, but in the gesture, she felt as close to him as she had when their lips had met.

Closer.

'What the boy said, about the dragon, I didn't mean…'

She did not want to know that he had said. She did not want to know any more of what this man thought of her.

She squeezed the boy and stepped away. Exhausted, his head drooped onto her shoulder and his eyelids sagged, weary.

Stella dared meet Rob's eyes again. 'Most children outgrow those shouting fits by this age.'

'He is not most children.'

She sighed, expecting again his argument that the boy should be abandoned. Instead, his brown eyes studied Wat, then returned to hers.

'He is lucky to have you. A boy like that... It would be easy for harm to come to him.'

'I know.' She squeezed Wat so tightly that he woke and lifted his head. 'Wat, listen to me. What did I tell you?'

'Always go home.'

'That's right. No matter what, whether you are scared or frightened or angry, you must not run off alone. Something could happen to you.'

'I be good,' Wat said, again, nodding at her this time as if he meant it.

'Be sure you are,' Rob said, in a tone that conveyed that the incident was over.

She turned away and smiled, knowing Wat's promise would not be kept, but grateful to Rob for trying. He'd learn when he had children of his own.

Somehow, the thought was not comforting.

Chapter Nine

He was glad, Rob told himself a few days later, that Johnnie returned so quickly with the head man of the Elliots. He'd been thinking too much of the Storwick woman. And with the Gregor fool in his arms, his thoughts had even turned to children. He needed to get married.

That would clear his mind.

Rob, Johnnie and Jock Elliot settled before the empty hearth in the public hall. Jock was of an age of his late father. It seemed unnatural to meet him face to face as an equal, each man head of a family with all the duty that entailed.

'Your father was a braw man,' Jock began.

'Aye.' No more to say. No way to admit he missed him without sounding like a boy instead of a man.

Silence fell. Rob looked to Johnnie, who leaned forwards to pick up the thought.

'So,' Johnnie began, smiling at Jock, 'you've a daughter of marriageable age.'

Rob tried to remember her. He must have seen her at some gathering. Had she been at his father's burial? Hard to say. He had seen little that day for the tears in his eyes.

'Aye,' Jock said. 'She's full seventeen summers.'

Rob frowned. 'So young?' Younger than his sister Bessie. Much younger than Stella Storwick, though that made no difference to him.

'Old enough to marry. Many are at her age.'

He knew as much. 'Can she cook?'

Johnnie glanced at him, but held his tongue.

'Lamb stew, bannocks, carrots. The kitchen is home to her.'

Carrots. Not his favourite. 'Fish?'

'Aye, fish, too.'

Dull, he thought, but useful. Exactly what he wanted.

'And she is healthy?' Johnnie asked.

'Never sick a day in her life,' her father said. He leaned forwards and lowered his voice. 'And a lovely lass, if a father may say so. Fair hair. Brown eyes. Full figured. Only missing two of her teeth.'

He swallowed. That should not matter. Not at all. He did not care if the woman was comely or ill favoured. He needed an alliance with a family and a marriage with a woman who could manage the household.

'And,' Jock continued, with a smile that revealed the teeth *he* was missing, 'we would be honoured to be joined to the Brunson's head man.'

Rob stood. To the head man. The only reason they would be considering the match. A woman who didn't even know him.

They want to claim they carry the son of the head man.

That was all she wanted.

And wasn't that what he wanted? he thought, with more than a twinge of guilt. He had asked no more of this prospective 'wife', than she had of him. A nameless body had been all he had wanted. Not a woman for her own sake, but only one to cook his food and order his house.

That no longer seemed enough.

As he left the room, Johnnie, sputtering, struggled to explain his brother's abrupt departure.

Stella saw Rob stride out of the hall, looking like thunder. She had learned enough of him now that she no longer assumed he was frowning at her.

It was the whole world he hated.

'Is there news?' she asked.

He glanced over his shoulder. 'We were speaking of marriage.'

Her stomach took a dive. 'Yours?' No reason that should matter. She looked at Rob Brunson, his expression as black as his name, and shivered. What woman would want to live with such a man? It would be a death sentence, a banishment to everlasting Hell to be tied to such a beast.

She would never survive such a thing. It was the worst fate imaginable.

He didn't answer for a moment, but his eyes took hers. And she thought he was trying to tell her something without words.

'Aye.'

There it was, then. She swallowed, hoping she could find her voice again. 'May it be a happy one.'

Something shifted, as if the rock hard expression shattered. 'Whenever it happens.'

She looked behind him. Another equally unhappy man was saying a few words to Johnnie as he stomped towards his horse. 'It is not—'

'Nay. Not now. It will not be that one.'

She closed her eyes in grateful thanks, ignoring the meaning of her relief.

When she opened them, he was looking over his shoulder at the stranger. 'And now I must fix the mess I made. Jock Elliot's kin have been staunch allies of the Brunsons. Until now.'

He turned his back on her and strode back to the man. Curious, she watched the two brothers. Johnnie had a hand on the man's shoulder, as if trying to cajole him into a better humour. Rob must have made one of his blunt statements and the man took offence. Well, her father would have raised a fist to any man who had spoken amiss of her, although, she realised now, her prideful attitude might have sometimes deserved it.

But Rob stood square before the man, and

though she could not hear his words, the angle of his head and the furrow on his brow suggested a spare statement about himself.

Admitting he was wrong.

At least, that's what the shock on Jock Elliot's face seemed to say.

Her relief slid into puzzlement.

She was no expert on Rob Brunson, but she could not remember him ever admitting an error before.

She turned away. Marriage to Rob Brunson. What woman would suffer such a sacrifice unless…?

Unless it was what she had been saved to do.

She wandered towards the tower, casting a casual glance behind her. If a Storwick were to marry a Brunson, would that mean peace?

Would that mean her father could come home?

If so, it would be worth any sacrifice. Even a lifetime with Rob Brunson.

Brunsons and Storwicks had married before, of course. Once or twice. Border law forbade it, but even the edicts of kings couldn't stop young lust. In the end, though, those couples had had to choose one side or the other.

And they had not been the head man of one clan and the daughter of the leader of the other.

The certainty of it settled on her like the fog on the hills.

Stella, God saved you for a reason. It must be a large reason. Something important.

That's what her mother had always said. And so she had expected a vision to come from God, showing her exactly what she must do. Perhaps like that maid in France, God might put her on a horse at the head of a great band of riders and ask her to lead them into battle, guiding them to a glorious triumph.

But as the years passed, no vision came. So she had grasped at the idea of crossing the border looking for her father. That was the biggest, most important thing life had ever asked of her.

Until now.

To bring peace to two families that had warred for generations. Was that her purpose?

She wondered, sceptical. It would bring no moment of public glory and triumph. This would be a harder, private sacrifice. This would mean putting herself at the mercy of a monster, day after day, for the rest of her life, spent in exile, forced to submit to his kisses.

The shiver that went through her was not entirely unpleasant.

But the certainty that grew seemed immutable. Why else would God have allowed her to be captured, but to turn the hard heart of this man to release her father and embrace her clan?

She straightened her shoulders. She did not know how she would do it, but marry Black Rob Brunson she must.

Or die trying.

Rob was certain, after he had choked on the taste of his swallowed pride, that now was not the time for marriage. Why had he even thought so? Ever since the Storwick wench had appeared, his thoughts had been muddled. Now was no time to be distracted by a woman, even a wife. He must get on and make plans with Johnnie and Carwell, prepare to deal with the King.

And the Storwicks.

They had surprised him, 'twas true. Perhaps they were cleverer than he had given them credit for. For it seemed the Storwick cousins, whoever they were, had decided to just let poor Hobbes Storwick rot in Carwell's castle and the daughter to do the same in his. And if they waited long enough, and took charge, what they wanted would become inevitable. They would lead the clan in fact until, after a while, no one but Storwick's poor wife would remember, or care, what had become of him.

Sometimes, life could be cruel that way.

The question was, when the time came, what kind of warriors would they be?

Johnnie and Cate had returned to the other end of the valley, carting some stone from the abandoned church to fortify their rising tower, half a day's ride away. Wed only a few months, they were eager for their own place, their own space. So Rob slept alone in his father's room again, living suspended, knowing that they would have to act soon, that the King would be coming.

He was sorry, now, that he had insisted that Stella stay here. He had become lax about guarding her, but she seemed so comfortable, as if she were part of the household. So as long as she remained within sight of the tower and took the boy, he let her outside to check the fish trap. As long as the lad was with her, he felt certain she would not run.

And if she did, it would make his life easier.

He was too aware of her, he thought, as he mounted the tower stairs late one afternoon. Where she was, what she was doing. She lavished smiles and hugs on poor Wat Gregor, and every once in a while, he would catch her studying him, as if she were trying to see into his mind.

Thank goodness she couldn't. Once in a while, she might have seen herself naked there and—

'Is there any word of my father?'

Her voice jarred him. She stood in the door of her room, looking as comfortable as if she lived there. 'Why would there be? Have you seen any messengers coming or going?'

She looked down. 'Cate told me she had seen him. I thought there might be news, he might be better...'

Hope, he thought. All we ever had most of the time.

He reached for her sleeve. 'I'm sorry.' And he wasn't sure exactly what he was sorry for. Certainly he had no regrets for anything he had done. And yet he was using those words now as he never had before.

'When did your father die?'

Her unexpected question hit him like a blow. He did not want to be reminded of his father. He did not want to be reminded of how she would feel if her father...

'August last.'

'How did he go?'

Rob shook his head. 'In his sleep.' Shame, to say the words.

'A lucky man.'

He stared at her. He had not thought so at the time.

She did not relent. 'And your mother?'

He shrugged. 'A few years before.' Two? Three? He was no longer sure.

'I've been fortunate,' she said. 'To have my family so long.'

Life was uncertain and merciless, especially for the weak. 'You've family still. You've a clan full of Storwicks.'

'It's not the same.' Her eyes met his. '*You* have a brother. And a sister. I've had just my parents.'

'There are days I would let you have them.'

Yet he smiled, as Johnnie might, knowing he did not mean the words.

And she smiled as if she knew he did not. 'My father and mother, no matter what happened, they thought I was special.'

There was that word again. As if it were some magic cloak that belonged to her alone. 'My father did not think the same.' Perhaps fathers of girls were more forgiving. He did not recall his father raising a hand to Bessie.

'It is not always a blessing,' she said. 'It is hard to know if you…' She let the words trail away. 'If you are good enough.'

He nodded. 'That I know. With my father, the answer was always "not yet."' *Not good enough to be head man.* There had been so much to learn. And now, too late for his father to teach him more.

'With mine, the answer was "you will be." They had expectations.'

'Aye. So did my father.'

Strange. Their fathers treated them so differently, but with the same result. *Am I good enough?* He would never have imagined that

Stella Storwick would wonder. She seemed to think herself quite better than them all.

'But they always believed I would fulfil them,' she said. 'In time.'

He wished he could say the same. He thought his father might live for ever, if only because Rob was unready to succeed him.

'And now,' she said, whispering to herself, 'there is no more time.'

No more time. One day, he woke up and he was alone.

The same could happen to her, she knew too well, and it might be his fault. Once more, he found himself flopping like a fish on the line, tempted once again to let her go to the man in time to say farewell.

He found himself wanting to comfort her, this woman who was not only alone here, it seemed, but alone even among her own kind. It made them feel akin, in a way, for as head man he was alone. No matter what Johnnie could do, at the end of the day, he was alone. Would another body next to him in that bed help?

And then he had crossed her threshold, stepped within her room, put his arm around her, felt her nestle against his shoulder without fear, and when he looked down, she was lifting her face, her lips close enough to kiss.

And he did.

Not like before. Not with desire and possession mixed. This time, it was like a benediction. A blessing. A sharing of the sorrow and joy and poignancy of life all distilled in a touch.

A nibble, a little more. And then, mutually, they parted.

The kiss had spoken.

Just as those glances between his parents once had.

Rob had never trusted words, and while he didn't want to, he had to trust this.

And its message made him shake as no battle ever had.

Stella's heart thumped against her chest. She could hear it in her ears.

His arms still surrounded her, strong as the wall around the tower. Strong enough that no harm would ever come to the woman he chose as his wife.

Up to now, they had shared only anger and desire and their differences.

This kiss was between two, imperfect, wounded people who might comfort each other. And as she rested, still, in his arms, hearing his heart where her ear rested against his chest, she could see days and nights and months and years, resting exactly so.

The thought should have comforted her. It did not. It made the fantasy of marriage to him too real. Not a vision of leading an army on a charging steed or of self-righteous sacrifice on an enemy's altar. Just a life with ebbs and flows. Mornings and evenings. Births and deaths. And someone to share it all.

She straightened. He dropped his arms, as if he, too, had just realised who, and what, they were. She stepped back, turned away and brushed off her skirt, as if she could brush away the closeness. Behind her, she heard him clear his throat, felt him square his shoulders.

'I should find Wat,' she said, still not ready to face him. 'Without me to look after him, something might happen.' How could she have been so careless? The boy might go exploring again. He might fall down a well…

'Stella.'

His voice commanded she look at him. She let her fear, her doubt and her anger fall away, and did. 'Yes?'

He wanted to speak. She could tell that much. Had learned to read at least some of his expressions. Pain. Regret. Yearning. She could see all that. Even that he might consider letting her go…

Or did she see only her own feelings?

And then he smiled. A small one. Rueful. One that said clearly there were things he would not say.

'Will there be fish for the table today?'

She nodded, as if that had been their conversation. 'Aye.'

And as he left, all she could think of was that they had built the fish trap together.

Chapter Ten

The kiss gave Stella pause. In his arms, it had all seemed real. Even possible.

Still, it was strange to walk the tower and the courtyard and to picture it being her home, to picture being Rob's wife.

When she had first come, forced to see the world from this side of the border, everything looked backwards, as if she was peering into her looking glass with the world reversed behind her. Even the sun rose and set in the wrong place.

She had expected to enter a world of evil monsters. Instead, she was surrounded by people who ate, slept and peed the same way her family did.

And given Willie Storwick, these people were probably nicer.

So although she told herself that to marry Rob Brunson would be a great hardship, it was not, strictly speaking, the truth.

The kitchen needed help, yes, and the Warrior Woman was as fierce as any rider she had ever known, but aside from that, and their accents, these people were not so different from her own.

Except that they did not hold their breath when they looked at her, waiting. They simply judged her on what was before them. The Stella of today, not some long-ago miracle.

And Rob Brunson, the man she expected to be as black as his name, was strong, silent, stubborn, and as devoted to his people as her father to his.

The world was a strange place indeed if she could see herself living in the Brunson Tower. But if she did, Rob Brunson could not deny his wife's wish to see her father before his death. Could he?

So, as May stretched towards June, she fell into the rhythm of the household. With Johnnie and Cate gone, Rob tended the sheep and she tended Wat and the fish traps.

And nothing more was said of kings or truces or her father. Yet something hovered, unspoken, as if everyone were waiting…

And one fine May day, she tired of waiting for a miracle.

She sat in her room after the evening meal, listening to the household quiet, hoping he would not make a late eve of checking the guards. The sheep and lambs would start making their way into the hills tomorrow, he had said, and he would be off riding more than usual.

When she thought he might have returned, she sneaked into his room, lit only by the leftover moonlight. Not for him the comfort of a candle.

He was standing, chest bare, as if he had been undressing for the night.

'What brings you?'

She kept her mouth shut. She would have to show him. To overcome his resistance with her body instead of talking. If she could join with him, then he would see.

She pressed her body against his, raised her hands and pulled his face down to hers. He could have resisted. Could have held her off, easily, but he didn't. Did he want it as much as she?

His arms tightened around her. He deepened the kiss. And she thought the answer must be *yes*.

Yes.

'Stella...'

His lips moved over hers, then explored the taste of her cheek, her ear, her neck, until his lips and hands seemed to be everywhere at once. And then, he took her mouth again, not gently, but with his tongue thrust deeply into her, meeting, fighting with hers.

No respectful kiss she had ever received was anything like this.

She felt its echo below her waist, felt the emptiness there that wanted him.

Yes, wanted him.

Had she come here, calculating, meaning to seduce him? She could no longer remember. Her body took command now.

And his.

She let her greedy hands slide from his cheeks down his neck and shoulders to stroke the skin of his back and then of his chest. Her breasts burned now, wanting to press against him, the muscles as hard as she had imagined. The shaft between his legs harder.

Did she know what came next, what to do? No matter. Her hands, her lips, moved of their own will, over his skin, to his waist, lower. She dropped to her knees, her fingers fumbled at his breeches, but he took her wrists, in that implacable grip, and pulled her up, then lifted her into his arms and laid her on the bed.

She closed her eyes, the better to feel, to sense him. From that first day, pressed against the ground of the hills, she had wanted this, wanted him over her, ready to possess her, to take her, to make her surrender as she had refused to do all these weeks.

She reached down to pull up her skirts and spread her legs and then reached for his hand, not knowing what else to do, eyes still shut tight.

Please.

He paused.

She opened her eyes.

For a moment, suspended above her, he was far enough away that she could see his eyes. No words. The man spoke little at the best of times.

He was not one to put emotions into words instead of action.

So she must act, too, not wait for her brain to talk to her in confusing riddles. She wanted her body to speak as his always did. Forceful. Strong. Unhesitating.

She grabbed his tarse and drew it to her, drew him to her, inevitable, impossible to resist.

If he gripped his teeth any more tightly, he would break them apart and swallow them all.

You can't. You can't. Not her.

But her touch made him as heedless and thoughtless as the young man who had kissed the girls who didn't want him, but only what he could give.

And why did this woman want him? To trick him? He did not know. But it was not for love. That could not be.

He pulled from her, feeling her fingers slip away, and he almost turned back. Almost shook it all off to bury himself in her and in forgetfulness. He wanted to take her, to brand her, to touch her so that she would never be Storwick again, so that she would belong...

He rolled off the bed, stumbled and clung to the bedpost. Belong to him? No. That must not be.

He searched for an even breath. This had been no gentle kiss or exploration. This had been the most primitive sort of desire. One that might make her think him no better a man than Scarred Willie Storwick.

But it had felt like more. Beyond. And that feeling was one he feared even more.

He staggered on his feet. On the bed, she pushed herself to a sitting position and tugged her skirt down to cover her bare legs, not looking at him. Her breasts rose and fell as she tried to catch a breath, with no more success than he.

In a moment, she would raise her eyes to his and he would have to face the hate in them again. Hate that these past weeks had almost erased.

He closed his eyes. 'I should not have…' Weak words, but the only ones he had.

The rustle of bedclothes ceased.

He opened his eyes.

Her expression was not what he expected. 'It was…' A large breath, then, 'It was not you alone.'

Aye. That was what had spurred him on. The woman had been hungry for him. Still was, judging by her eyes.

A match for his.

They looked at each other, making love without touching.

Don't let go of the bedpost, Rob me boy. Or you'll not be able to control what happens next.

No doubt there was something else he should say, but Rob was not a talker. Johnnie was the one who played with words. Rob believed that if a man was to do a thing, he should do it, not blabber on about it.

But if her body's desire mirrored his, he was facing danger strong as ever he had faced from a Storwick before, more treacherous than the point of a Storwick's pike.

She looked away first, swung her legs over the other side of the bed and stood. He let go a sigh of relief and looked about for the clothes they had flung aside in their haste. It gave him something to do. Put on a shirt. Tie a knot in the breeches. Flimsy armour, but the best he had.

She stood at the window, her back still shutting him out. 'Your room looks south, but clouds have covered the stars tonight. Will it rain tomorrow, do you think?'

He picked up a scrap of cloth. A handkerchief. Hers.

His fingers tightened on it. 'This will not happen again,' he said.

She whirled to face him. 'Will it not?'

He could not read her eyes. Anguish? Challenge? Did she thrust her breasts towards him in temptation?

She was the one. She was the one who had kissed him.

'Next time you knock,' he said. 'I'll not open to you.'

But she had opened to him. Her legs, white and soft and willing. Her hands trying to guide him home... The memory still hot enough that he was at the ready all over again.

She must have sensed it. Walked around the bed that separated them, hips swaying, until she was close enough for him to catch the scent of her and be lost all over again.

Her arms snaked around his neck. Her fingers tangled in his hair and pushed his head to her lips...

'No!' He grabbed her hands, capturing her wrists and held her at arm's length.

Flushed, she seemed angry enough to breathe fire. Or was that desire instead?

'What do you want of me, woman? Do you think to lure me to your bed so you can accuse me of defiling you?' Although touching her had not been defilement, but connection deep as life.

She shook her head and he sensed some shame there.

He struggled to put his head in command of his body. 'Or do you just plan to kill me in my own bed?'

'I thought…' Now she was the wordless one.

'What?' He shook her arms, getting her to meet his eyes again. Who was this woman? He had thought her arrogant and idle and useless. Yet no one could have been more caring with Wat. But never, ever, had he thought she would be so brazen as to force herself on him, though he had thought of her in his arms, and in his bed, more times than he wanted to admit. Even to himself.

She only shrugged and shook her head.

'I'm taking you to your room,' he said. 'And if you ever try this again, I will lock you up below.'

That was the only threat that had ever seemed to frighten her. She didn't seem to fear anything else. Even him.

Holding her wrists with his left hand, he opened the door a crack. The corridor was empty. He strode into the hall, swinging her behind him, opened the door to her room and shoved her across the threshold.

Just before he closed the door, she looked up at him and he could see the hunger in her eyes again, physical, and more…

He leaned towards her, words, conviction fled again, lips parted, matching hers.

At the last moment, he forced himself to swerve and leave his kiss on her cheek before he closed the door.

And then, he realised he still clutched her handkerchief in his hand.

Chapter Eleven

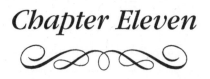

Stella found no peace in sleep. Nor in dreams.

Her body still burned, whether from shame or desire she could not say.

Her plan had gone horribly, horribly wrong.

All her self-righteous talk of sacrifice was a lie. She wanted him. Wanted him still. Wanted him with some kind of wild, reckless abandon that had stolen a simple plan and run roughshod over her intentions.

This was not the noble martyrdom she had expected. Nor was it the glorious, but hard-won victory she had long thought her mission would be.

It was carnal lust.

But she had not been alone in that. He wanted her just as strongly. She knew it. Felt it in his body's response. Strong and forceful, yes, but not cruel. Wanted her, wanted to take her, and yet it was all hunger and urgency, he, too, near helpless against the tide.

But not quite.

He had been the stronger. He had been strong enough to stop.

She was not sure why. Not because he respected her, surely. His disdain had been clear from the first. But there had been a struggle, behind his eyes. Something he had no words for. Something that could only be captured in the softest kiss.

As if there was some reason he didn't want to speak. Or couldn't.

And for that, she did not know whether to love or hate him.

Love. Where had the word come from? She had intended marriage and peace between the families, never love. Love meant his needs would be as important as hers. Love would make her vulnerable, even helpless…

And the next moment, she realised what she must do.

Leave.

There was no more to discover here. Her father was being held far away and Black Rob had refused all pleas to let her see him. She must flee before her father was lost to her for ever.

Before she succumbed to one more kiss in Rob Brunson's arms.

Coward. He's the one you must escape.

Soon. Now.

Tomorrow.

The next morning, once Stella was certain Rob had left to ride his rounds, she strolled across the courtyard, carrying her salmon-catching sack, full of other things. She entered the kitchen and scooped up a bannock or two, bidding Beggy gudday.

'Wat gets hungry,' she said, stuffing the food cakes in her hanging pocket.

She spared only a careless glance for the kitchen as she left, as if her eyes only tripped over it instead of bidding it farewell.

On the way out of the gate, she waved to the guard as if it were an ordinary day, smiling, hoping he would not stop her.

He did. 'Where's the lad this morning?'

'He'll be along.' Though she hoped not. She did not think she could bid Wat farewell without tears. 'I just need to check the weir.' As she did every day. 'By the nightfall, we'll have salmon, I hope.'

She said it with a smile.

Fortunately, Sim Tait was a man who liked salmon. And who underestimated how far a woman could get without a horse.

She strolled slowly, swinging her sack, and her hips, from side to side. If he watched her, all he would see was a woman enjoying the early summer sun.

'Wait, wait!' Wat's voice. He was running to catch her.

Ran right into her arms and she hugged him. Hard.

She had not wanted to see him this morning. Not wanted to come face to face with the child she'd come to love. At least with Wat, she could admit it.

She was crying and rubbed the tears away. 'Now, Wat, I think Beggy just put some fresh bannocks in to bake. Please go back to the kitchen and wait until they are done and bring one back for each of us. Can you do that?'

He nodded and turned to run back to the tower.

And if I am not here when you come back...

No. She could not say that. Couldn't give even this poor child a hint. Maybe they would think she had drowned in the stream...

'And, Wat,' she called, waiting for him to stop and listen. 'What did I tell you?'

'Always go home.'

She nodded, choked and waved. 'Now go.'

She watched until he was back inside the walls surrounding the tower, then, she dipped over the rise and down to the edge of the stream and let go a breath, knowing she was out of sight.

The water ran merrily this morning. She glimpsed a flash of silver scales and held her breath. A fish?

It did not matter. She would not allow it to matter.

She tiptoed towards the water, so as not to startle the fish. Then, she looked at the construction of twigs and sticks that she and Rob and Wat had built.

Putting down the basket, she searched the

ground for a tree branch heavy enough to do some damage. Then, hefting one with both hands, she waded into the stream and swung it at the weir, madly as if she were Wat, obsessed with repeating the same thing, over and over.

Madly as if she could destroy her feelings for Rob along with the weir they had built.

Water sprayed and splashed until it dripped from her hair and skirt and she did not have to sort the tears from the stream that snatched the twigs away and sent them merrily careening towards the Solway Firth.

Then, she wiped the damp hair from her forehead, lifted her skirt and her basket, and headed west.

Rob's first thought, when he returned that night and discovered her gone, was that he'd been a blind fool and had no business being head of the Brunsons.

The guard had last seen her mid-morning. Hours ago. But he had become used to her coming and going to the stream and had thought nothing of it.

But Wat? Wat should have missed her.

'Why didn't you tell someone, Wat?' He wanted to shake the boy.

'Always go home.'

He sighed. That's what she had told the boy, trying to keep him safe. At least that poor fool had had the sense to listen.

'She ran away,' Wat said, tear tracks on his cheeks. 'She doesn't love me any more.'

Rob knelt in the dirt, feeling too big and too awkward and too much like adding his tears to Wat's. 'It's not you, lad.' He patted the boy's shoulder. Faint comfort, but all he knew. 'I'll find her. I'll bring her back.'

Yet which of them was the bigger fool? Rob had been foolish enough to trust her more than he ought because he had let her turn his head. Last night's kisses had no more meaning than any woman's. She kissed him in order to get what she wanted.

No other reason. No other feeling. A woman could wield a kiss with the same skill a man could shoot an arrow from his latch.

Had he really thought a Storwick would stay?

He rose and looked behind him. Today, he had ridden to John and Cate's end of the valley to admire their rising tower and they had returned with him to stock up on oats and ale. As they gathered to plan next steps, he felt a moment's gratitude they were at his side.

'We'll need Belde,' he said, as the three of them went back to saddle the horses again. Cate's great hound would be able to track the woman as if she had left a trail of stars. Rob could find his way through these hills in the dark as if he had the sight, but who could guess which way a frantic woman alone might run? Without the dog, he might waste hours.

Cate and Johnnie exchanged glances. 'If she went home,' his brother said, 'she'll near be there by now.'

It was barely five miles to the border. She'd be well over it and nearly to Bewcastle by now. But something might have happened to her. She could be hurt, alone, with dark falling...

He swung into the saddle.

'Do you mean to ride into Storwick lands? I'll not let Cate go with you.'

'Then let me have the dog. I'll go alone.'

'You know little of tracking with the dog,' Cate said.

'I know all I need to.' He held out his hand.

Johnnie looked at Cate. The beast was hers. As would be the decision.

She sighed. 'She's a woman, for all that she's a Storwick.' Tying the dog's lead, she handed the strap to Rob. 'What do you have that's hers?'

He drew out the kerchief, stuffed into his bag, with no explanation of why it was there, grateful that Cate and John held their tongues, if not their glances. Given a whiff, the dog strained at the leash and led him out of the gate and to the stream.

South. Home, then.

But first the dog went straight to the river bank where they had relaxed when the weir was complete. The water sounded different today. He peered closer, and in the light of gloaming, he could see only the bubbling ripples.

No dam of sticks.

No fish trap.

Only a few broken twigs bobbing on the foam.

Johnnie, slower to mount, now joined him. Grateful as he was to have his brother at his side, he could not even raise his head to look at him. Not until he had strangled his feelings.

She destroyed it. The thing they had built together.

But the dog was tugging on the leash and trying to turn him downstream. Why? This stretch of Liddel Water was as narrow as any further west. A good place to cross if you were going south to the hills.

Johnnie reached for the leash and Rob released it. 'Pause, Belde.' Only Cate could control the beast, but he paced, waiting for John to say 'fetch' again. 'What's in that direction?'

And suddenly, it was clear where she had gone. And why.

'Her father,' Rob said.

'Is she daft enough to head to Carwell Castle?'

Daft enough? 'Aye.' Any woman who walked right across the border and into enemy land would not hesitate to strike out for the castle on the coast, even if she knew nothing of how to get there.

'That will take her straight into the Debatable Lands.'

Where even the Border Laws did not apply.

He should let her go. Because she was Storwick. Because she had fooled him. Because his life had been nothing but trouble since she arrived.

But he turned Felloun to the west and held out his hand to take Belde's leash.

'Then that's where we'll go.'

Because she was a foolish woman alone and because he had promised Wat he would bring her back.

And because he could not let her go.

How long? Stella thought, as the sun drifted lower and the outlines of the hills became stark against the sky. *How long until he discovers me gone?*

At first, she had run along the bank of the stream, but once she was beyond sight of the tower, staggering, she sank to her knees and took the time to catch her breath.

Just a little further and she'd be clear of the hills. Just a little further and the land would flatten and the stream she was following would become the border. Just a little further and she could wade across the water and be on Storwick land.

But that was not her plan.

If her cousins cared not enough to offer for her, she cared not enough to return home.

It was her father she wanted to see now.

She stood and let her eyes follow the stream as far as she could see. Somewhere near Canonbie, it would join with the River Esk. Beyond there, the river would skirt the Debatable Lands and, eventually, reach the sea. If she followed it that far, then she could turn north and parallel the coast. Carwell's Castle would be there, somewhere. A two-day ride, if she had judged correctly. But to walk, when she was uncertain of the path?

Days.

She took the first step. Then days it would be.

Each step doubled her doubts. Stella Storwick, saved by God to do what? Not to save her father or to expose the Brunsons' weakness so her family could defeat them. Not even to marry and bring peace.

No, Stella Storwick was not even fit to cook or clean or run a house and be an ordinary wife.

She cleared her throat against threatening tears. Not for leaving Black Rob Brunson, a man who earned every dark syllable of his name. It was only Wat she regretted leaving. A boy no one else seemed to want. A boy who might fall down a well and never be missed. Maybe to his life, she had made a difference. Or could have.

Too late now.

Her steps slowed. How far had she come? How far had she to go? And how long could she survive on two bannocks?

No more thought, no better plan than the last time. Foolish enough to think she could simply flee and God would provide.

No, not that foolish. She had not thought that at all. All she had thought of was to run and whether it was to reach her father or to flee Rob Brunson she wasn't sure and did not want to be.

When she stepped on soft earth, her left ankle twisted and she dropped like a stone.

Only a misstep. Just stand and keep walking.

But when she put weight on it, she winced. She was striding no more. Not even walking. Just hobbling, and with each step, the ankle throbbed anew, worse each time.

Carwell Castle was not days away now. It was as far away as Heaven.

She sank to the ground again, grinding her teeth against the pain, and pummelled the dirt.

What are ye good for, lass?

Could she do nothing right? If God had saved her, He must regret it now.

She looked around, trying to assess how far she had come and whether he would be able to find her. She had made good time in those early hours, and tried to, just in case they didn't wait for Rob before they came after her. The land was flatter here, and the hills more distant. Fewer places to hide.

It would be dark soon.

And there would be no moon tonight.

Belde, given the scent of her, did not hesitate for miles. Stella was not, after all, hard to track, for she hugged the path of Liddel Water, and a woman on foot could go only so far.

The light faded. The dog's nose was just as sharp, but the horses were less sure-footed. Some said the reivers could ride in full dark. Near true, and Rob's eyes were better than most, but the horses were accustomed to the tracks through the hills, not the land by the river.

Belde strained at the leash now.

Near. She must be near.

He pulled Felloun to a stop.

'Stella!' he yelled, no longer caring what he sounded like, or who else might hear. Then, silent, he listened for an answer, but heard only wind and water.

Johnnie paused beside him. 'Let the dog go. She's close.'

He did, slid off the horse and followed deeper into the trees until the dog stopped, tail wagging, and poking his nose to sniff her all over in triumph.

Rob could see why she had not answered.

She was slumped against a tree, looking near lifeless, and shivering, though the night was not cold. 'Stella?'

She turned her head, as if she could not face him, but when he picked her up in his arms, he felt a tear hit his hand.

So he bit back the harangue he had planned and carried her to the waiting horse. His fault. His weakness. He had indulged her, trusted her and this was the result. Once they were home, he would make sure she could never put herself in such danger again.

In his arms, Stella's fear faded.

She had worked near this stream, waded in these very waters, for the past few weeks, but that had been in daylight. In the dark, the sound of water brought the familiar fear with it.

She curled against his chest, cherishing the rhythm of his heart and of the horse's hooves. Just a few more miles, just a few short steps and she'd be back in her room in the tower. She'd be given a mug of ale and a fire would be built and she'd be tucked into her bed, her ankle wrapped, and she'd be safe again.

Out of the dark.

Tomorrow she would face Rob. He'd be angry...

She woke as she was lifted off the horse, transferred from one pair of arms to another and back, and carried inside. Rob's voice rumbled in his chest, barking orders.

But it was not until she realised that they were not mounting stairs did she lift her head and open her eyes.

She was in a small, dark room. And she could hear the echo of water on stone.

'No.' She could barely choke out the one word.

Someone bustled around her, blankets materialised. Her ankle was wrapped. Food and drink were set within reach of her hand.

Someone brought a candle and set the holder on the floor and then she could see exactly where she was.

Fear stole the rest of her voice until all she could do was cling to him, eyes wide, her nails digging into his arm. If she did not let go, he would not leave without her.

He pried her fingers away and a guttural whimper escaped her throat. 'Please.'

Was that pain in his eyes? No matter. The set of his jaw held no mercy. 'This is the only room with a lock, so here you'll stay.'

She waved her hand. 'But I cannot even walk.'

'You say. Do I believe you?' He shook his head and rose. 'Not again.'

He took a step towards the door and his foot knocked the cover of the well ajar. She closed her eyes, certain the next sound would be his scream and a splash as he plummeted to the bottom on the well.

Silence.

She opened her eyes.

Only a sliver, only an inch. She pushed herself away from it, but her back was already pressed against the stone.

She looked up. His back was to her. Another step and he would be gone. 'Please.'

He paused. And she released a breath. He would not be so cruel as to leave her here alone.

But instead of turning, he spoke over his shoulder. 'I trusted you and you made me a fool. You'll not charm your way out of *this* place, so it's here you'll stay.'

He shut the iron gate.

Chapter Twelve

Stella did not sleep that night.

Or, at least, she thought it was night. He had left the lit candle behind, but the flickering shadows terrified her as much as the darkness.

The gap where the well cover did not shield the opening yawned like a monster's maw. The few moments she drifted into dreams, they were of a dragon, emerging from the shaft to clasp her ankle and drag her towards the well, closer, closer…

This time there would be no escape.

She told herself the well was safely covered. That a sturdy wooden barrier stood between her and the deep, dark shaft that ended in the cold of underground water. But that thought, repeated over and over, was only the weak voice of reason.

No match for the remembered scream. No comfort to the soul of the little girl who had fallen down a well shaft so long ago.

And all the assurance she had developed since, all the reassurance that God had saved her, rang hollow. Saved, perhaps, but in error. Only temporarily. The well would have her at last.

There is nothing special about you, Stella Storwick.

That was only the wish of a mother and father, of parents with only one child.

She pressed her back against the wall, as if by pressing hard enough, she would force the wall to hold her safe. Far enough from the well so that she could not touch it, even by accident. Finally, afraid to move, afraid she might trip or fall or somehow end up in that damp darkness again, she slumped down to the ground and curled into a ball, legs and feet tucked underneath her, just beyond reach of death.

Alone in the dark with nothing but doubts.

The creek of the iron yett as it swung open was part of her dream at first, sounding like the scrape of iron on stone as they had tried to reach her, frantically. A voice—was it her mother's? Her mother had wept and prayed.

This voice did not. This was a voice she could not dream.

'Rob Brunson, are you daft?' The Warrior Woman's voice.

A woman's hands, small and gentle, settled around her shoulders.

'I was thinking to be sure she didn't escape again and bring the Storwicks across the border to murder us in our beds.' Implacable words. Did she hear regret beneath them?

She opened her eyes to see Cate's brown ones, feeling the woman take her measure. This was one who had no love for the Storwicks. For good reason.

Stella struggled to hide the night's fear behind her pride. Too late. Cate had glimpsed it. And now, something else coloured her expression. Understanding.

She put a shoulder under Stella's arm. 'Stand. I will help you.'

She struggled to stand upright, keeping her eyes averted from the big round hole in the middle of the floor and from Rob Brunson. She had begged him, like the basest coward. How could she face him now?

Yet now, as daylight filtered into the room, fear eased its grip and she risked a glance, first, at the well.

The cover was ajar, yes, but no more than a finger's width.

Then she lifted her eyes to meet Rob Brunson's brown ones.

And the fact that his looked as sleepless as hers was small consolation.

Rob crossed the room in two strides and supported Stella's other side. 'Your ankle is not strong enough to stand on.'

But he could not meet her eyes as he said it. He had never seen Stella like this. No longer arrogant or prideful, but terrified, as if she had spent the night alone with spirits.

'She's frightened half to death,' Cate growled, and Cate was a woman who knew something of fear.

My God. What had he done? Only tried to protect her.

No. It was himself he had tried to protect by putting her out of his reach.

She took a step and staggered. Cate struggled to catch her weight.

Rob scooped her up again, holding her close to his chest and striding up the stairs, leaving Cate behind, eager to put Stella back in the room where he should have put her all along. Inside, he laid her carefully on the bed.

She immediately tried to rise, but he put his hands on her shoulders and held her down. Fight had returned to her eyes, but the fear remained.

'You locked me down there. With…that.'

'There's something about it,' he said, trying to pull the threads together. From the first, she had shivered against it, but he had not thought of that last night. He had only thought of locking her where she could not run. And where he could not reach her. 'Something about that room.'

She turned her head and he saw tears again.

He pulled his hands away. 'You should have told me.' He knew nothing of women. Only of fighting. And of fighting his weakness for this one.

She sat up in the bed. 'I tried.'

'Am I to see into your mind, then?' Pacing the room now, not wanting to leave her, but reluctant to come too close.

She bit her lip and cast down her eyes. 'It is… hard to speak of.' Then she raised her eyes and he saw again her pride and her privilege. 'Particularly to a Brunson.'

'Aye. That, I understand.' As hard as it would be for him to say he was sorry. Doubt, weakness, that was to be shared with no one. Especially not with an enemy.

A small smile, then. Forgiveness? More than he deserved. Not a cruel man, he reminded himself, but careless, aye, which had been just as bad.

He sat on the edge of the bed and put her hand in his. 'Tell me anyway.'

'I can tell you only what I've been told.' She took a deep breath. 'I fell into a well. No one saw it happen and when someone finally missed me, they could not find me.' She swallowed and he could see her breath, the short, shallow pants of fear again. 'They could not find me for a long time.'

'You were at the bottom of a well alone?'

She nodded.

Bruised. Hungry. In deep water. So many tools that Death could choose. Even a warrior would shiver. 'How old were you?'

'Two? I'm not sure. I remember nothing of it but the story as my mother told it.'

But he could tell her body remembered it. Her body remembered it all over again as she was locked up with a well overnight.

And it had been his fault.

Grown men died. That was to be expected. Children, even babies did, too. That, he had never got used to.

But Stella Storwick was very much alive. 'But they found you. You survived. You were lucky.'

'More than luck. A miracle.'

He raised his brows. 'A miracle.'

'That's what my mother called it. She prayed to the Virgin Mary and the Virgin saved me.'

He did not want to call the woman a liar, but miracles were scarce on the Borders. 'Yes, but who pulled you from the well?'

'An angel.'

She said it in the same, straightforward tone that she would have announced that dinner was ready. 'You saw an angel?' The Angel of Death, perhaps. Maybe she had seen him just before—

'I didn't, but my mother did. She prayed for a miracle and the Virgin sent an angel who lifted me out of the well.'

Bedtime stories for a child, he thought, yet parents create our world with their tales.

He set that thought aside.

'So you see,' she continued, looking at him with troubled eyes, 'she knew that God had saved me for a reason.'

'Why?'

'I don't know. No one knows.'

Rob was not a churching man. The Archbishop of Glasgow had cursed all Border reivers to hell and Rob returned the favour. But if God truly had saved this woman…

He let go of her hand. It wasn't seemly to touch a saint. Or ask one to cook. 'Is that why your life was made so easy?'

Her eyes turned hard. 'You think that being saved made it easy on me?'

He paused. He had not thought of it at all. 'What do you mean?'

'All my life, people looked at me, like you are

now. Watching. Waiting. Expecting me to do something worth being saved for.'

Just as everyone looked to the head man, waiting for him to produce a life for them out of stingy ground.

She grabbed his hand again. 'And last night, I wondered again whether I had been saved in error.'

'What do you mean?'

'Why would the Virgin save *me*? What am I supposed to do? I cannot part the seas or turn water to wine or multiply loaves and fishes. I can't even catch a blasted fish!'

'Well, you try living up to the whole line of Brunsons back to the First!' He gripped her fingers now, his voice poised on the edge of a shout. Angry with himself. Or his father. 'I'm supposed to know everything, to do everything, to save everyone. And when you came, I couldn't even put a fish on the table!'

She blinked. Then, slowly, she reached up to touch his cheek. 'All that being looked up to. It's hard on a body.'

Then her expression dissolved, not into tears, but into a smile just short of laughter.

He grabbed the hand against his cheek and turned his lips to it. She swayed closer and they nestled together. 'Ah, Stella, we're a pair, aren't we?'

She was the one who reached out to him. He reminded himself of that later.

It didn't matter. They melted together as if it had been destined to be, as if two so opposite people must ultimately join and explode.

He explored her face first. Those sharp bones, the pointed chin, the wide eyes green as grass. But quickly, he wanted more. He wanted her skin. He wanted to hear her breath in his bones.

He wanted this woman. Who she was inside, beyond that foolish name of Storwick.

He stumbled on the thought. If she was more than *Storwick*, what was he beyond *Brunson*?

The question, tied to words, floated away. He wanted no more words. Tricky, slippery things. He wanted grunts and pants and moans deeper than language. Nothing of words now. Nothing of thought. Only breath and skin and bones and the sound of desire.

She knew nothing of lovemaking, not even

enough to fear it. She had not kissed many, that he could tell, which made his fierce possession of her lips even sweeter.

Aye, she was a special one, his Stella. He had never tasted her like. She gave herself proudly, but fully, as if she knew her worth and knew he, too, was worthy.

I don't know what I am supposed to do, she had cried.

But with this, somehow, she did. Aye, she did.

And he let the wordless madness take him.

At his touch, the rest disappeared. There was no world but this bed, this man, this joining. All new, but perfect and complete.

More perfect and complete than she had ever hoped to feel.

All the ways she had failed, all the things she could not do, none of those joined them here. Gift or sacrifice, this, she was created for.

To join with this man.

To have a child.

The thought floated away when she pressed her skin to his.

But later, when he had spilled his seed, and he slept, she thought of it again.

So this is it, something whispered, inside of her.

She had heard other whispers before. Whispers about Willie Storwick. Based on those, she had little interest in the things men and women did.

And few men were interested in her, either. She thought, in those days, that their tepid kisses were all there was. Perhaps she and Rob were alike in that way, too. The men she knew saw her as untouchable. The women Rob knew saw him only as the head man. Each separated from ordinary connections.

But not from each other.

Who pulled you from the well?

She lay in his arms, trying to think back one more time. Trying to remember the day she became…different.

What she remembered was fear.

She knew what had happened only because she had heard the story so many times. It was painted in her mind like a Biblical tale of loaves and fishes or Lazarus, rising from the dead.

You were a headstrong child, her mother

would say. *Even then. Always going off without a thought.*

And her mother would go on about how she had suddenly discovered Stella missing, combed the sleeping chamber and then the hall and then the stairs and the stables and on and on, finally realising the worst must have happened and looked down the well.

And every time her mother told the story, the length of time Stella was missing and the hours her mother had prayed became longer and longer until, finally, she had been missing forty days and forty nights before she was found.

How long had it been? She didn't know. And now she was not sure that her mother did, either. There was only the story, retold, more real than truth.

Stella remembered nothing of being saved. Nothing of the angel. Had he been fair? Had his wings touched the ground?

Once, she had told her mother he had brown eyes, but her mother had said that was impossible. She had seen him clearly and his eyes were blue.

So, much as she had tried, Stella remembered

nothing before her life began anew. A life for which she had been saved from danger she still feared in her bones. A life now under God's watchful eye. A life that stretched out towards some predestined, but invisible, end.

Rob's warm weight nestled next to her, more solid and certain than anything she had ever had in her life. What would it be like, having this man beside her every night?

And how could she even ask or imagine such a thing? A Brunson and a Storwick? It would take an act of God to bring peace between them.

An act of God.

Such as the one that had saved her.

She looked down at the dark lashes fanning his strong face. Maybe she had been right. Maybe this was why she had been saved. She had run the last time, unable to reconcile passion and duty. Now, the very thing she had fled welcomed her home.

The thought brought a sigh of relief. If that were so, it would not be wrong to love him. Only that for which she had been saved. Her purpose, finally, in life.

Or was she simply putting words in the mouth of God?

But there was a rightness she felt here. Something she had never felt anywhere before. Not just in his arms, but in the tower, with Wat. It was somewhere she was not special. Somewhere she could be ordinary, accepted, close, without those awestruck distances people kept.

Words rose up, those she had not been able to summon when the passion flamed hot.

He controls you. Now that he knows, he might lock you with the well again until you are mad with fear. He is strong. He could hold you down, make you submit...

There had been no force here but the force of their feelings. Only fierce hunger, his, hers. Only uncontrollable yearning across a chasm so deep that one false step would send them both tumbling to doom.

Yet somehow, she felt as calm as she had ever felt. After all the days and years of feeling others' eyes on her, wondering, waiting for her to do...something, here in the enemy's tower she felt as if her skin belonged to her at last.

Could God have saved her to lie with a

Brunson? Her mother, when she discovered all this, which she must, inevitably, would mourn unto death.

And yet, and yet, he was a strong and respected leader. One who would do anything to protect those in his care, as her father always did. And she had seen him be gentle with the child.

She had even seen him lift a wounded young lamb with care.

But more clearly than any of that, she had seen that he was alone.

Just as she was.

Except not now. Finally, she no longer felt alone.

Rob held her in his arms, tightly, as if nothing could change as long as he never let her go, as if he could keep her tight and safe in this bed, in this room, until the end of time.

As if he did not have to rise and face a world in which he had loved a Storwick.

Her even breath said she slept.

He opened his eyes without moving, afraid to wake her. She lay, peacefully, wrapped in his arms, arms he did not recognise. They could not belong to a Brunson. No man with Brunson blood could love a Storwick.

Who you love is who you are. And if he loved a Storwick, that meant he was not the man he had thought himself.

Not a Brunson at all.

It must have been what his father had feared, all along. That he was weak. Unworthy of the name.

He sat up, abruptly, waking her, and rose, stepping away, so she could not touch him.

So he could not reach for her.

He paced to the window, half-expecting to see Storwicks ready to breach the gates because he had been lured into bed and away from his duty to the land he loved, waiting outside, patient, for him to recover his wits.

And yet, now, apart from Stella, he felt alone again. Felt the isolation that had been his life, always, never fully recognised until, for those few moments, it was gone.

He turned his back on the valley and faced her. 'We will not do this again.'

She looked at him with a level gaze, calmer than he would have expected. 'Why?'

One word. And he was disarmed.

'Don't play words with me.' He was not a man who fought with words. Silences and swords were his weapons. He did not know how to articulate all the reasons he should not have shared a bed with Stella Storwick…

But a half-smile curved her lips and her eyes were halfway between dreamy and calculating. 'Words? Words are too weak for this.'

She threw off the covers and limped across the distance he had tried so desperately to hold. Then she wrapped herself to him as if he alone could keep her living and lifted her lips, trying to reach his again.

He gritted his teeth. The body whose strength had always been his pride was suddenly a feeble vessel, unable to resist this woman. Even his brain was muddled now. To hold her had become a burden, but when she relieved him of it, he had chased the length of Liddesdale to bring her back.

'Do you think,' he began, struggling to speak, 'that if I take you again I will let you go?'

She leaned away so she could meet his eyes. No calculation in hers. No pride. 'I think, that if you take me again, neither of us will ever let the other go.'

He did take her then. Arms around her, lips on hers, she, kissing back, and he had little more than one coherent second to wonder whether he was as demented as the Gregor boy, to worry about what would happen if his seed took root in her—

The knock on the door saved him.

'It's Cate' came the voice from the corridor. 'And Wat.'

Stella's eyes widened. 'Just a minute.' She limped back to the bed, straightening her chemise, reaching for skirt and bodice.

He, too, reacted as if battle threatened, donning his clothes swiftly, pulling up the covers.

'The boy,' he said, when she was settled on the bed again, her ankle on a pillow. 'He thought it was his fault that you left.'

Pain, regret, flashed over her face. Then, she lifted her chin. 'Come in, Wat.'

The door opened and a short, blond bundle streaked to the edge of the bed and lifted his arms. Rob lifted the child up so he could sit by

Stella and the two of them hugged, silent, for a long time.

He left them, closing the door as he joined Cate outside.

Finally, separated from Stella by stone and wood, he could think clearly again. Aye, he'd been as daft as poor Wat. Only his limitations were not so obvious.

And more dangerous.

Cate raised her eyebrows and studied him, waiting.

Clear enough to his brother's wife what had gone on in that room. Cate and Johnnie had shared the same bed once. Nothing he could say to excuse or explain what he had done.

But Cate could wield the weapon of silence, too.

'Go chatter to Johnnie if it pains you to hold your tongue,' he said, finally, unable to stand her silent scrutiny.

She shook her head, but glanced down the stairs, towards the well room. 'I hope you told her you were sorry.'

He turned to stone as she walked away. He had

not. And of all the things he regretted about this morning, that was the worst.

Stella smiled as Wat burrowed close, not lifting his head until she had sat and rocked him for a long, long time, wondering what to say.

Finally, she said nothing at all.

At long last, he raised his head, tear tracks dry on his face. 'I'm sorry. I won't be bad again. I promise.'

Rob was right, Wat thought it was his fault.

'It was nothing you did, Wat. I wanted to see my father and he…' She must keep it simple. 'He is far away.'

'Did you see him?'

Far was a mysterious distance, apparently. 'No.' She pointed to her ankle. 'I hurt my foot and couldn't walk the rest of the way.'

'And that's when the laird saved you!' He bounced on the bed, as if he had discovered the story's end and liked it.

'In a way, yes.' Not in a way for a child to know.

Wat jumped off the bed and tugged on her hand. 'So let's go fish, then.'

And that's when she remembered. 'Wat, something happened to the weir.'

'What?'

Innocent faith she did not deserve. 'I…' He needed truth. Just not the whole truth. 'I broke it.'

'On purpose?' Puzzlement on his face.

She nodded. 'I'm afraid so.'

'Why?'

'I was angry.' Remembered fear and anger surged through her again. Aye, she had feared her feelings for Rob near as much as she had feared the well. And with as much reason. 'It was wrong of me.'

He sighed and shook his head, rolling his eyes in an expression of long suffering he must have copied from his mother. Then, he patted her hand. 'I forgive you. Promise you won't do it again.'

She stifled a smile. 'I promise.'

'Promise you be good?'

Ah, what would that mean now? 'I promise.'

His smile returned. 'Then we'll build another.'

'I'm afraid I can't.' She wiggled her ankle, then winced, wishing she had not.

'Will you be better tomorrow?'

Would she? Already, her body craved Rob again and she was impatient for the night. But nothing had been settled between them.

'I don't know, Wat,' she said. 'We'll see.'

Chapter Thirteen

Rob spent the day thinking he must send her away. Should have let her run and good riddance, just as he had once suspected. She had his brain and his body twisted and tangled and the only thing that seemed certain was the most dangerous of all.

If you take me again, neither of us will ever let the other go.

As long as she was here, as long as she was close enough for him to see her and touch her, as long as they slept under the same roof, he would take her again.

Yet he'd not let the Storwicks have her. Miracle or no, they had not wanted her enough to offer for her. What kind of reception would she find at home? And he had been foolish enough to give her the run of the household. She knew enough about the tower and the men to hand her family the intelligence they needed to penetrate even his new defences.

Yet where else could she go? He would trust Johnnie and Cate with her, but their tower was not yet finished. Jock Elliot's tower was strong and the man trustworthy, but since he had refused to wed the daughter, well, now was not the time to ask more of the Elliots.

No. There was only one place to take her. The very place she wanted to go.

If Stella had felt fear in the dungeon and comfort in the bed, she felt something quite different as the day went on.

Rob had disappeared. She could not walk well enough to leave the room. Suddenly all the rightness she had felt slid away. The day was endless, but whether it was because she was confined to the room or because she did not see Rob it was hard to say.

Wat stayed with her for a while, but he was young and full of energy and there was little there to entertain him. When he became crabby and bored, she let him go, with stern warnings to be careful.

Near midday, there was a knock on the door. 'Come.' Difficult to speak. What would he say first?

Not Rob, Cate, carrying a bowl of porridge. 'I thought you would be hungry.'

Surprising to see such kindness from a woman who hated her. Yet nothing from Rob. Had he spared a thought for her at all?

'I thank you,' she said, expecting Cate to set it down and leave.

Instead, she wandered the room while Stella ate a few spoonfuls and regretted again the destruction of the weir.

'He did not mean to be cruel,' the woman said, at last.

'Cruel?' What could this woman know of what Rob had done to her?

'When he locked you in the cell.'

She shook her head, as if it didn't matter, thinking of the first time Cate had taken her measure. A woman Willie Storwick had touched? That woman would know real cruelty. And how to fight it.

Cate did not seem to expect an answer. 'He is not a man who is at ease with a woman.'

The very word made her smile. 'He is not a man at ease with the world.'

Cate did not turn away, but seemed to study her and, courage in hand, Stella returned the gaze. Steady. Waiting. Wondering what the woman was thinking and why she had come.

Finally, something like a nod. 'You might be good for him.'

Her eyes widened. Surely she misunderstood. The Warrior Woman could not be thinking of a marriage between Brunson and Storwick.

Could she?

She cleared her throat. Cautious. She must be cautious. 'What do you mean?'

But having said her piece, Cate turned towards the door, shaking her head. 'Never thought to see the day,' she said, just before the door closed.

Leaving Stella to wonder whether Rob had any inkling of what Cate thought. And whether he thought the same.

Hours passed before Rob appeared again.

She had hobbled to the window and back, her

ankle throbbing when she put weight on it and when the blood seemed to rush around it. She was well and truly at the man's mercy now and the fault was her own.

And she tried not to ponder the fact that her emotions were as captive as her body.

She recognised his knock this time and that he waited for her permission before he entered.

When she saw him, the pace of her heart, the gasp in her throat, told her that her treacherous body had succumbed to him all over again.

She waited for him to speak, waited while he devoured her with his gaze, glad for both their sakes that he clung to the door, the full length of the room away.

'We leave tomorrow.'

Not the words she had expected. 'Are you taking me home, then?' The thought did not bring the joy it would have last month.

He shook his head. 'To see your father.'

Relief, hope, gratitude, love, swirled through her veins and propelled her the few steps across the floor. She reached out to touch him. 'Thank you.'

'Don't thank me yet.'

She pulled back her hand. Yes, they could be too late. Her father could be dead, but at least he had tried.

He looked down at her foot. 'Can you ride?'

At the thought of hours dangling on the back of a pony, her ankle began to pound. Well, no one would pamper poor Stella here. Not a cruel man, but one who never questioned duty. She should do the same. 'Aye. I'll manage.'

He nodded, now avoiding her eyes. 'Tomorrow, then. First light.' Turning away, closing the door…

'Wait.'

He stopped, quickly, as if with the word he had reached the end of a rope, and looked at her again.

'Did last night mean nothing to you?'

Yet she could see by his eyes that it did. 'Would you have me betray what I was born to?'

'There was no Brunson in that bed last night. No Storwick. There was only a man and a woman. And if your body lied to me, well, then…' She inhaled. 'Then you are not the man I thought you were.'

'And just who did you think I was?' Pride and

anger mixed in his words. 'You've known all along who I was.'

'Aye, you're a Brunson. But you're also an honest and stubborn man who'll kneel to no one.'

'Including you.'

She bit her tongue. He was a man any woman on this side of the border would be proud to have. How could she have been foolish enough to think the man would ever be forgiving enough to marry a Storwick? Only another daft idea she had dreamed, hoping to find her purpose in life.

'And after I see my father? Then what will you do with me?'

He sighed. 'Carwell Castle first. After that…'

The sentence had no end.

Rob left Johnnie to guard the tower and took a dozen men with him for protection, not only from an attack, but from the temptation to take her again. Well, not from temptation, but from the chance to act on it.

And by the time they rode across the bridge into Carwell Castle, he was a man whose teeth had been ground to a nub from holding himself in check.

He had sent a man ahead, telling himself that this trip was no soft-hearted surrender to Stella. He needed to confer with Carwell before the King arrived and Hobbes Storwick was too ill to be moved. That was the reason for the journey. Nothing to do with his weakness for Stella Storwick, physical or emotional.

But after? His choices would become more difficult. Best to leave her there, he thought, as the huge, three-sided castle came into view. Carwell Castle could house a dozen such prisoners. Leave her with her father, let her bid goodbye to the bastard and let Carwell be burdened with her.

Inside the vast, triangular courtyard, the red hair of his sister Bessie was the first thing he saw. Wordless, she hugged him. Was she slightly thicker about the middle? Perhaps, but if Cate had not told him, he would not have guessed she was with child. He stifled a moment of envy when he saw the glow on her face. It became brighter every time she looked at her husband.

Carwell clasped his arm, a warmer greeting than he deserved. Or wanted.

But there was no time to waste. 'Is he alive?' he asked Carwell.

'Aye.'

Then, Stella was beside him. 'Where is he?'

Rob looked down at her ankle, frowning. She should not have dismounted without help.

Bessie stepped forwards, not wasting time on niceties. 'Come.'

He watched the two women walk away, dark hair next to red. Stella's steps were slow.

'You should not be walking,' he said. It was a large castle. She'd be near lame before she reached her father.

In two strides, he reached the women and swept Stella into his arms. No struggle. No argument. Instead, she drooped against his shoulder, a gesture louder than words. The warmth, the weight of her felt right against his chest.

He tightened his grip and looked at Bessie, ignoring the question in her eyes. 'Which way?'

His sister smiled. 'You're a good man, Rob Brunson.'

He shrugged. 'We had no chance to bid our father farewell.'

Bessie nodded and led the way.

* * *

Stella rested against Rob's chest as he walked down corridors and up stairs, until they came to a room as far from the entrance as possible.

He let her down, gently. 'Are you ready?'

She looked at him then, hope and confusion in her eyes. And his. 'Thank you.'

Turning to the door, she straightened her shoulders.

'You should know,' Bessie said, softly. 'Sometimes he is not…here.'

And she swung the door open.

They had housed her father high in a tower, with a window that let in the sound of the sea. As Bessie closed the door, Stella saw only a wan figure, lying in a canopied bed, under blankets too warm for the May air.

A few steps and she was beside him, sitting on the bed, wrapped in comforting arms as if he were still the strong father, she the little girl he protected.

They separated, finally, and she sat up so she could fill her eyes with him. Gaunt. Pale. Weak. The body of the father she knew had left him. But the spirit, ah, that was still there.

His hand, held in hers, seemed made of bones so brittle they would break if she squeezed. Only then did she really understand the truth of it.

He is dying, she had told Rob. But she had thought only of separation. All the way here, she had planned to lay the problems of the squabbling cousins in his lap, trusting he could solve them still if only he came home. The family needed him. If the cousins could be forced to pay a ransom, he could come home...

And things could be as they had always been.

'They let you come,' he said, finally, each word a stone to be lifted.

None of that mattered now, all those foolish things she had thought. 'Aye.'

'More than I would have done.'

'A man you don't meet every day,' she said, whispering the words, 'for all that he's a Brunson.'

He frowned, not wanting to hear. 'Your mother?' Few words. Enough.

'Well, when I saw her last.' A lifetime ago. Had they even told him that she had been so foolish as to be captured by Rob Brunson? No need to, if he did not know. 'Praying for you.'

'And you?' He squeezed her hands now. 'God still watches you.'

Never a question in his mind.

Only questions in hers. Questions near erupting into screams.

What do you expect of me?

She took a breath, then let it go. One more thing too late to ask. So she nodded.

His smile was reward enough. 'When you go home, tell them—'

'I won't leave you.'

'After...' He gasped for breath. 'After I'm...'

Gone.

She had known. She had told Rob as much. But face to face and knowing she would lose him... 'No!' Squeezing his hand without caring if it hurt him. As if she could hold him tightly enough to keep him alive.

'What were you thinking, girl?' he asked, finally. 'To get yourself captured like that?'

Ah, so they had told him. Now she must confess the foolishness of the younger self she had been just a few weeks ago. 'I thought that I had been saved so I could save you, so I crossed the border to look for you.'

His gaze seemed to drift to Heaven. He turned his head away.

'Father?' She gripped his shoulders, trying to force his attention. 'What *does* God want me to do?'

There was no answer but his breathing.

Rob faced Thomas Carwell across the table in the man's working chamber, both of them frowning.

'You received the King's message,' Carwell said. 'He's coming to the Borders next month.'

'I've heard of the man's coming since he escaped Angus and sent Johnnie home last year.' Rob scoffed. He had sent Johnnie to bring the Brunsons to fight the Earl of Angus, but Brunsons did not borrow other men's battles. Even a king's. 'We haven't seen him yet.'

'This time we will. He finally forced Angus to flee the country and now he turns his attention to us. He is scheduling days of justice and bringing enough men to impose his will by force, if the law won't serve.'

Rob shrugged, trying to keep his mind in this room instead of the one in the tower.

'Aren't you worried, man?' Carwell snapped. 'He's already named you an outlaw and ordered me to bring you to Edinburgh.'

An order, to Carwell's credit, he had not carried out, making him an outlaw, too. 'And you're worried because he'll treat you as a Brunson?'

'I'm worried because I've a wife carrying my child.'

'He'll be a Brunson, then.' He, for Bessie would, of course, bear a son.

A frown, then a sigh. 'Between you and the King, he has little choice.'

Bessie with child. No matter that she had married a Carwell and her son would be Warden of the March and bear his name. Brunson blood would run through his veins. That was the way of it. Family was given, not chosen.

Rob leaned forwards. 'So tell me more, about this King of yours.'

Behind Stella, Bessie entered, quietly. She moved around the room calmly straightening the blankets, then offering a sip of water to the man lying in the bed. After, she washed his face with a soft cloth.

Small things. Things Stella should have done.

She must be a kind woman, to do them for an enemy.

'When is your child due?' Stella asked.

Bessie straightened and put her hand on her belly, eyes wide with surprise. 'I've told only family. I didn't think anyone could see…so soon.'

Stella shrugged. It took envious eyes to see so clearly.

Then Bessie frowned. 'You won't curse the babe, will you?'

'Of course not!' Stella shook her head, shocked that Bessie would think so. Still, a Storwick must seem alien to this woman, as a Brunson had to her a few weeks ago.

Bessie went back to her washing and Stella stroked her father's other hand. He did not respond.

'He sleeps and then wakes,' Bessie explained, in a whisper. 'Sometimes, for a while, he speaks as strong as any man.'

Her words were witness. She had seen the cycle many times. 'You've been kind to him.' Strange enemies, these Brunsons.

'I lost my own father not ten months ago. Suddenly.'

And just like that, Rob was head man. 'Were he and Rob close?' There had been no son for her father. And no one named to step in when the time came. Would things have been different if she had not been a girl?

Silent, Bessie assessed her. Stella felt as if she were being judged to see if she were worthy of the answer. 'My father spent his life training Rob, to be sure he would be ready. Everyone knew he was chosen.'

Chosen. Just as Stella had been. Rob, at least, knew what he was chosen to do.

Time drifted away, borne on the sound of waves at the window. Bessie came and went and still Stella sat by the bedside. Late in the day, her father woke again and she saw in his eyes the father she knew and smiled.

'This Brunson,' he said, voice ragged with pain. 'What kind of man is he?'

Her body burned at his words. 'Judge him yourself. He is here.'

His eyes closed and he nodded. 'Bring him.'

She rose, trying to disguise her limp as she hobbled towards the door and stepped into the corridor.

And bumped into Rob.

'Have you lurked here all the day?' Her words were sharper than she had intended, uncertain whether she should be touched or angry, wondering what he had heard.

He shook his head. 'I thought you might need…to go somewhere.' He looked around. 'For women's things.'

A smile rushed to her lips before she could stop it. So long ago it was, when she had first set foot in Brunson Tower. 'Thank you for thinking of it.' She nodded to the small room tucked into the wall. 'There's a garderobe right here.'

He flushed and looked down at the stones of the floor.

'But I'm glad you've come.' She drew herself up and was Stella Storwick again. 'He wants to see you.'

That quickly, he became Black Rob again. 'Why?'

'Who knows why?'

'I've nothing to say to him.'

'He's a dying man. Maybe he wants to say something to you.'

He stood, silent, saying neither *yea* or *nay*. She let him take his time. Stubborn as a Brunson. Even the English knew the meaning of it.

The last of the sunlight turned the corner and left the hall in shadow. 'Will you meet with him, then?'

For me. That, she would not say.

Still, he knew it. 'You want it so much?'

She did, unsure why it mattered to bring together these two men who could only hate each other. Except that she...she loved them both. A thought quickly stifled.

'He does,' she said. 'And he is my father.'

Teeth clenched, Rob stepped into the room.

Here was Hobbes Storwick. A man he had hated all his life. A man he had fought against. A man who had torched his home. And yet, here he lay, pale against the bedclothes, reminding Rob of nothing more than the way his father had looked the morning they had found him dead in his bed.

No difference then, in the hours surrounding death, between a father and an enemy.

Storwick opened his eyes and Rob saw hate, strong as it should be. Comforting. That, he understood, and his gaze returned it in kind.

He stood beside the bed and looked down, waiting, while Stella hovered at the door.

Her father looked at her. 'Leave us,' he said.

Rob turned his head, expecting her to argue, but before he could catch her eye, she had closed the door behind her, leaving him alone with his worst enemy.

'You have my girl.'

So that was it. Dolt that he was not to have realised it. It was a father he faced now, not a head man. 'Aye.'

'Due to her own foolishness.'

Rob could not stop his smile. 'Aye.'

'I want you to let her go.'

Let her go. His first rush of feeling was not anger. It was emptiness. 'Why should I do that?'

'You don't need her now. I'll be dead before dawn.'

All the arguments he had made to himself over

the past weeks lay like dead leaves at his feet except the one Hobbes Storwick must not know.

That there might be a child.

'They do not want her back. Did you know that?'

The man closed his eyes and pain creased his forehead. Not pain in his body, it seemed. 'Her mother does.'

Rob could not argue against that.

Storwick lifted his hand, but could not form a fist. 'Nothing but weaklings left.'

Had his father felt the same? Had he lain on his bed, shaking his fist in fear of what would happen to the Brunson family after he was gone?

This man did. And, as far as Rob could tell, with good reason. No one had stepped up to take the reins.

To think of it another way, Hobbes Storwick had not trained anyone to do so. So was the fault his or theirs? Not perfect, then. Maybe no head man could be.

Even Rob Brunson.

Hobbes Storwick still spoke. 'There was weakness in the blood. Willie—'

'Willie Storwick deserved whatever death he got.'

'And worse. He was no longer ours.'

He had told Rob as much the very Truce Day that the man escaped, but Rob had never fully believed it. 'Hard for a man to do.'

'I would not have him around my girl.'

The thought of him doing to Stella what he had done to Cate made Rob want him killed all over again. No wonder Johnnie had been so fierce.

'He did us all a favour, the man who killed him.'

Or the woman. Or even the dog. But those were not his secrets to share. 'Aye.' Strange to agree with the man.

'So you'll take her home?'

'I did not promise.'

'Did you take her, then?'

Rob opened his mouth. No words came out.

'Aye. You did.'

He felt as young and foolish as he had been when his father took the strap to him. Standing there, thinking he had fooled the old man.

Storwick sighed. 'I should kill you myself.'

An empty threat now. 'But I won't, because I'm asking you to take me home, too.'

He looked at the man, pale as grey snow, and felt for him. Like his father, deprived of a death in battle. But his father, at least, had been buried as a Brunson should. With family all around and his son to honour him by adding a new verse to the Ballad of the Brunsons.

What if it had been his father, held on the English side of the border, dying? Would Rob have wanted him dropped into a mudhole and left, unmarked and unmourned?

I'm asking you… What it must have cost the man to say that.

'Die in peace, old man.' No question that he would say yes. One warrior honoured another. 'I'll take ye home to rest.'

Because you are her father.

Storwick's lips curved and he closed his eyes.

Rob's promise must have given him permission to die, for Hobbes Storwick did not live through the night.

Chapter Fourteen

Numb, Stella let Bessie coax her out of the room where her father lay dead. 'Sleep now. I will prepare him.'

Prepare him for what? But her tongue was too weary to form the words.

There were things that should be done, but someone else had always done them. Now, when she should have shouldered the load, Stella knew nothing of how to prepare the body or ward off the Devil.

Silent, she let Bessie lead her through the halls to a room where a bed beckoned. Beside it, on a small chest, oat cakes lay to hand ready to eat when she had strength and stomach for them. Rob's sister did not ask, but helped her undress and prepared her for bed as if she were a child and then tiptoed to the door.

As sleep crouched, ready to pounce, Stella summoned the strength to raise her head. 'Thank you.'

Bessie nodded.

'And is Rob...?' *Where is he?* That's what she wanted to ask. Tied by an uncertain mix of hate and attraction, they had rarely been apart the last weeks. Always, she seemed to know where he was and when she would see him again. Now, in her grief, he was the one person she wanted to see.

'You've no family here and your father's body should not be left alone. Rob sits with him.'

The door closed.

Her father had died surrounded by enemies, far from home, yet an enemy acted as kin.

What would happen now? Would they throw him to the waves?

And her last thought before sleep was that Rob would not allow it.

Rob did not see Stella the next day.

Bessie, the sister who cleaned up after everyone else, swept in to prepare the body. Carwell's steward found a cart to carry the corpse and pro-

visions for the men while Carwell sent word to
the English Warden to let them pass in peace.

Rob shook his head. 'And do you expect Lord
Acre to ensure the safety of a band of Brunsons?'

Carwell sighed. 'I trust him less than you do.
But he's a Storwick ally. He'll let the man come
home.'

But after Hobbes Storwick's body was safely
delivered, well, there would be no promises.

Bessie emerged, weary, and leaned against her
husband, such a natural gesture Rob flinched to
see it. 'She still sleeps,' she said, as if she knew
Rob wanted news of Stella.

'An unhappy end,' Carwell said. 'But now you
can take them both home. Leave her to her family. It will assuage the warden. And the King.'

They don't want her. Not the way I do.

He stayed silent. Let them think Stella would
be going home. Perhaps by the time they got
there, he could summon the strength to leave her.

She rose, finally, uncertain how long she had
slept. Night and day had merged as she sat by
her father's side and in a strange place, it was

hard to know whether the shaft of sun on her floor came from west or east.

She dressed and forced herself to open the door, surprised to see Rob sitting on a bench. How long had he been waiting?

He rose, his eyes silently assessing her as if she were a bastle house he was about to raid. She stood straighter and lifted her chin, certain she looked as weary as she felt, then tried to smile.

'Are you ready to travel, then?' he asked.

So soon. Life moved on after death. 'Where do we go?'

'Your father asked me to take his body home.'

No resentment in his voice, for all her father had been his enemy. Both of them, warriors before all.

'And what…?' She struggled against unwelcome tears. *What will happen to me?*

She did not complete the question. She knew the answer.

He would take her home, where she belonged. The whole misadventure would be over and she would never see Black Rob Brunson again.

* * *

Slowed by the cart that held her father's body, the journey back took longer than the crazed ride to the coast. Near Kershopefoote, Rob sent the rest of the men home to Liddesdale, leaving only the two of them to escort her father's body the rest of the way.

'Do you not fear an attack?' Stella asked, as the rest of the riders disappeared.

'I do not want your people to fear my intentions.'

Logical, yes, but she knew he had put himself at risk. The capture of Rob Brunson would be as much of a coup as the capture of her father had been.

Yet he risked it in order to bring an enemy home to rest.

'And what would happen to your people if…?' She could not say *if something were to happen to you*. Could scarcely think it.

He looked up the valley, not at her, when he answered, 'They would have my brother.'

Ah, even in this, he had thought of his people's future. She wished her father had done the same.

They continued on the Scottish side of the

water until they were out of sight of the truce village. The rustling of the trees and the rush of the water brought back the night she had fled.

And all the reasons why.

He led them into a small clearing, sheltered by budding spring-green leaves. 'We'll rest here tonight. In the morning…' he nodded to the south '…we'll cross into Storwick land. You'll see home before day's end.'

He helped her dismount and she stood easily, her ankle near healed. She spread blankets and drew water while he fed the horses and built a small fire.

Tomorrow. After tomorrow I will never see you again.

She struggled to bite back the words. Since he had walked from her room, he had become Black Rob again, stronger than she, once again the distant enemy he had been that first day.

A lie. The first time he had touched her, she had burned.

If you take me again, neither of us will ever let the other go.

But he would. She was sure of that now. Yes, she had seen the caring, the fire, in his eyes when he looked at her, but tomorrow, that would not matter. Tomorrow, he would deliver her into the waiting arms of her mother and the rest of her family, then he would mount Felloun and ride into the hills, away from her sight, away from her touch…

If her cousins didn't kill him first.

Whether she had been saved by God or was just another lost soul, the one thing in life that she wanted was within reach of her hand for only one more night and she was going to take it. Even at the risk of having his seed take root. If God blessed, or cursed, her with a Brunson babe, well, He would have to bless her with the strength to bear it.

She walked up the bank from the stream, glad that coming darkness could disguise her desire until she was closer, until neither of them could escape.

She moved with purpose, not with seductive languor.

But he knew.

Crouched before the fire, he looked up, stood, raised his hands to ward her off, but when she lifted her hands, tangled her fingers in his dark hair, pressed breasts against his chest and lifted her lips to him, there was only a sound. Growl. Moan. Cry of an animal in anguish.

And then he took her lips.

He had tried. God knows he had tried. But in the end, faced with her desire, he was as weak as he had feared.

He wanted her. Wanted her all. Wanted her now. Wanted her as if he could devour her and thus make her part of himself.

So they could never be separated.

Neither of us will let the other go.

He would. He must. For her sake. But, in truth, he would never let her go. She would be seared on his skin, embedded in each heartbeat.

He let the last thought go. Tomorrow. All that was for tomorrow.

This was tonight.

At first, all he wanted was her lips. Lips he had denied himself for days. Soft. Warm. Sweet. He took time, nibbling and tasting and teasing with his tongue. Tracing the bow of the top lip, perfectly balanced by the full pout of the bottom lip. Then more. Inside her welcoming mouth.

Open to him. All open. All giving. All wanting and taking.

He curled his hands around her head, marvelling at the perfect shape of it. Holding her closer so he could drink of her. Letting his fingers trail the sharp curve of her jaw until they joined where her chin jutted proudly before her.

And she, hungry as he. Loving with the desperation of goodbye. Of for ever. He was the one ready to slow, to savour, to love all night if they could because the time would not come again.

His hands felt so large. He tried to be gentle. Tried not to overwhelm her, because he was broad and strong and eager, so eager that he feared to hold her too tight. Feared he might break her with loving.

So he let his fingers move, slowly, gently, down her neck, her long, white neck, and to the front of her throat where he could feel the rumble of desire, sound without words.

Eyes. Eyes again. He pulled away just far enough to drink in the sight of her. Oh, he knew what she looked like. Fell asleep every night dreaming of green eyes and tumbling dark hair and the curve of a thigh he had seen but once.

But now, eyes closed, lips parted, languid with desire…aye, that was an image he would carry to the end of days.

She opened her eyes. In the gloaming light filtered through the leaves, he glimpsed desire darkening her eyes.

His lips parted. He should speak. He should tell her—

She raised a finger to his lips. Touch soft as silence. And then, he devoured that, too, and she was pressed to him again.

Stella did not want to speak. She did not want to think. She wanted only this act, this feeling. *This is what I was born for.*

As if her body knew, wiser than her mind.

She searched for the ties to his jack-of-plaites vest. Shielding him from harm, it also blocked her from the warmth of his chest, from the sound of his heart. And somehow her bodice disappeared. Soft air caressed her breasts, followed by his fingers. And she no longer had to fight thought, for she no longer could form words.

Tugging at his arm, she pulled them on to the spread blankets covering a carpet of bluebells.

The sweet, wild scent of crushed flowers stroked her skin and mingled with the smell of leather.

Wanting all of him at once, she left his lips to explore the skin of his shoulder, soft cover for strong muscles that shaped his arms and back. Greedy now. Touch and taste. So much of him still mysterious. So little time…

But all this night.

She pulled back, leaning on her elbow, to savour the sight of his chest, letting her fingers discover each curve as her eyes did.

Until she pulled back, his lips and fingers had moved, unceasing, across the terrain of her, steady and silent as the ponies navigated the hills. Yet knowing, always, how to take the next step. Even in the dark, a reiver's pony never faltered…

Deprived of her, his eyes opened, first with a flash of regret. But when he saw her face, with a smile that could not be contained, he shared it. Then, his fingers stroked the hair from her temple, his eyes tangled with hers, and the wind sighed, content.

'I will love you, lass. All of my days.'

She struggled to keep her smile steady, not

to think of all the days they would be apart between now and death. But this, this perfect moment, she would remember always.

'Show me, Rob Brunson,' she whispered. 'Show me deep and hard and long enough for us both to hold until the grave.'

Rob had taken her before, but reluctantly, fighting against his body, his heart, thinking he should not and so never relishing each moment.

Now, he did.

Now, he must create a lifetime of memories in one night. Tomorrow, he must let her go. She knew it as well as he. But this one night, they would have this always.

He started with his eyes, needing to see her before sunset stole the last of the light.

The dark hair, near as black as his own, that framed her brow. Fair skin a contrast to the strong bones of her cheek and the curve of her jaw and the narrow chin and the full lips. The green of her eyes no longer discernible as the shadows fell.

She smiled still, and he realised, belatedly, that she hoarded her smiles as much as he did. So as he saw this one, he echoed it, broad and unreserved. And as he did, hers shifted, turned the corner between delight and desire.

And that he echoed, too.

Fingers, next. He wanted to touch all of her, from top to toe and back, so that he would remember always. As he began, she reached for him, but he picked up her fingers, kissed them and pressed them against his lips.

'Shhhhh.'

He wanted no distractions.

He reached for her again, and this time she let him trail his fingers down her neck, then down the edge of her cross's chain until he reached her breasts, one for each hand, matched, yet one slightly different from the other. He cupped them, feeling their full heat, then gently pinched each nipple, switched hands, and did it all again. He would know, for ever, even in the dark, which was the right and which the left.

Her skirt was still tied on and she helped him push it off, along with the petycote. And when he saw the skin of her, white yet full of secret shadows, he thought he might never breathe again.

Eyes and hands explored together and he

thought, though God might strike him dead for it, that if some miracle had saved this woman to do something special, it must include making love.

A hipbone interrupted the curve below her waist, much as her collarbones created hills and shadows above her breasts. The closer he came, the more secrets her body seemed to keep as darkness wrapped itself around them. As it did, he closed his eyes and let his skin see her instead, shoulder to centre and lower, pressed against each other so tightly that he was sure there would be an imprint on his skin when they parted. And glad of it.

But much as he tried, his body no longer wanted to wait. Last time, he had let desire drive him. He had entered her fast and quick and deep as a night raid. This time must be different. This time must be long and slow and as deep as for ever.

He pushed himself up on his arms, trying to see her eyes before the light was truly gone. She must see him, meet his gaze, so she would see, so she would know…

But night had come and there would be no more glimpses. No more green meeting brown.

Eyes and fingers had looked their fill. Now, it would be lips.

She reached for him again, and he twitched his hips away, knowing that if her hands caught him, he would have no defences. With his tarse safely beyond reach of her fingers, his lips began to journey anew, starting at the place where her hair sprang from her head, kissing his way to her temple and down her neck, pausing in the hollow of her throat for the joy of hearing the guttural sound of her desire again.

Now he let his tongue roam freely, drawn to the tip of each breast, delighted to hear the soft keen of her craving.

She waved her hands, tangling them in his hair. 'Now. Now.'

He chuckled and flicked his tongue against her and shook his head *no*.

But he hurried now, down to the rise and fall of her hipbones, and then further, to the secrets hidden where her legs joined her belly, eager to find a new way to love her.

Now he could taste her indeed, sweet to his

tongue as the scent of the flowers around them. Eager, wanting to please her before he took his pleasure, he licked and dipped and plunged and played and each different touch made her shudder anew, until the wordless growl become a happy cry of release.

And as each ripple shuddered through her, he felt the pleasure shoot through him as well. Aye, he was so much a part of this woman he could feel the pounding of her blood and the grip of her body as if they were fully joined.

Oh, Robbie, me boy, he thought, with his last coherent breath, *how are you going to live without her?*

Stella did not sleep that night. Impossible as it seemed, there was always another way of loving to discover. She would not stop until they had found them all, every one of them, so she could take them out, one by one, as the years went on, and remember.

But all her dreading did not delay the day. She looked up and could see the outline of the trees, distinct against the pre-sun sky.

They lay in each other's arms, silent and still, as if watching the approach of the end of days.

And then, amidst the dark quiet of the dawn, Rob opened his lips and sang.

She had heard him sing before. He was the Brunson gifted with the voice, they had told her. So many nights, after supper, someone would take up pipes or bow and Rob would sing, his voice deep and strong. He would sing as if the song was enough, as if he led the people with his voice alone.

And lead them, he did. They would join him in songs of war, blending their voices with his until they swelled with the same united thunder as the hooves of their horses when they rode the hills.

She had shivered, then, for she could feel the rumble of battle in those notes.

But this was a song he had not sung to the men. It did not echo with the rhythm of the hooves, pounding over the hills. It did not carry the beat of war.

This melody lilted, surprisingly so, for the voice he brought to it.

Brave and true and strong she was
And special of her clan
A woman sought, a woman found
She wed that Brunson man

Brave and true and strong she was… A woman she would like to be.

'You've not sung that before,' she said, when the last note had faded. Afraid to ask him why.

He shrugged. 'It's one of the oldest of the Brunson ballads.'

'Of the First Brunson?' That name she knew. Impossible rival.

'Of the woman he loved.'

Loved. The word streaked through her, as sharp and as strong as lightning. She had heard all that in the words, in the voice, in a song that seemed to speak more powerfully of love than the words he had spoken.

She swallowed. 'Who was she?'

He shook his head. 'All we have is the song.' Then, a soft smile. 'Maybe she was the one. The one who saved him.'

'What did they call her, this woman?'

'It was strange. The First Brunson had no

name, or none we ever heard. But she did. They called her Leitakona.'

'What does that mean?'

'Woman looked for. And woman found.'

Chapter Fifteen

As they road into Storwick land, morning spread across the sky, achingly blue, the sun casting shadows in what Stella once had thought was the proper direction.

The family tower rose in the distance, gradually growing taller with each clop of the horses' hooves. All familiar to her, the land of her childhood, no longer looking like home.

When they reached the tower, the walk bristled with men carrying long bows, poised to let their arrows fly, with puzzled expressions on their faces.

Rob looked at her, waiting. This was her home. It was her place to speak.

'I have returned home. And I bring Hobbes Storwick to be laid to rest on his home soil.'

Her two cousins emerged from behind the wall of archers. 'And who is with you?' Oswyn said.

'I am Black Rob Brunson,' he roared beside her, for once unwilling to hold his tongue. 'Head man of the Brunson clan. I come in peace to bring your leader home to you.'

'Are you the man who killed him?' Humphrey this time. And neither had given the men an order to put down their bows.

'I am not!'

Stella lifted her hand, afraid he might lose his head at the insult. 'You all know well that my father was on his final journey when he was taken. He asked Rob Brunson to bring him home and you will not harm him for fulfilling Hobbes Storwick's last request. Now let us in!'

The men lowered their bows. Her cousins whispered to each other and, if she could interpret their expressions rightly, started to argue.

Then the gate below them opened and her mother rushed out, trailed by a few servants.

The servants ran ahead to lift her father's body from the cart that had borne him all the way from Carwell Castle. Stella dismounted and threw herself into her mother's arms.

Home.

She heard the hooves behind her and twisted away from her mother to see Rob turn the horse, ready to leave.

'Wait!' She stretched out her arm.

If he rode away now, he would leave her an empty shell. In all the hours of last night, they had never faced the truth of this moment, never planned how they would say goodbye.

She was not even certain he would heed her, but he paused. Then, before them all, he met her eyes. One look. Everything words could not say. As brave a thing as either of them might ever do.

Her mother gripped her arm, as if trying to tug her home, but Stella did not turn away from Rob. 'It is because of you he came home at all. You honoured him by your act. Let us honour you. Stay with us to see him buried.'

Stay with me. Just a little longer.

His gaze left her to flicker over her mother and the line of bowmen on the wall. Brave, she knew. He could face death and never flinch.

Was he brave enough to stay with her a few more days? Brave enough to face goodbye all over again?

His eyes returned to hers and all the rest fell away. 'If ye like.'

She let go her breath. Another day. Or two. Or three.

Rob cursed his weakness. To stay would only make it harder to leave later. Here, there would be no kisses, no touches, no joining. Only the agony of seeing her within reach of his hand, yet out of his grasp.

He no longer had to watch her to know where she was, so he let his eyes roam the Storwick stronghold. He knew the shape and size of it. Larger than the Brunson Tower. Smaller than Carwell Castle. Knew its vulnerabilities and its strengths and had come up against both in more than one attack, but always from the outside.

Three months it was since his men and Carwell's had swooped down with fire and spear and taken Hobbes Storwick captive, yet holes in charred straw still sagged where thatched roofs once protected the outbuildings.

The sight unsettled him. He knew what they had done, of course. Had done it on purpose. But coming to the compound as a guest, no matter how unwelcome, and seeing the destruction gave him pause.

But it told him more than that his emotions had changed. Three months was long enough for roofs to be repaired and walls cleaned. Weaklings, Hobbes had said, of the squabbling men on the walk. Truth was all around him.

Hobbes Storwick had not groomed a successor, as Geordie Brunson had. And now the Storwicks had no leader.

Home.
Stella walked through the gate, trying to match the word to the place. *I am home.*

Yet this yard was strange to her now. She expected to hear Beggy humming off-tune at her cooking. Or to see Wat run up to take her hand.

But something else was familiar. Something she had not missed in her time away.

The way they looked at her.

She had nearly forgotten the way everyone kept a respectful distance, as if God had placed her in a bubble to make them keep their distance.

Rob Brunson had had no such qualms.

Even now, he walked close behind her, as if he

might have to protect her at any moment, though he was the one in danger.

The memory of last night swept over her. His flesh, pressed to hers, the scent of his skin, the way she had writhed beneath him in joining…

She lifted her chin, certain her cheeks had coloured with the thought. She refused to remember the closeness of last night. Not here, while Humphrey and Oswyn were staring at her, waiting for proof that she was some sort of prophet.

No. She was not the same woman who had called this place home.

Her mother came closer, drawing her from Rob's side, and Stella met her eyes, full of questions and sorrow.

She wanted to say he had not suffered at the end. She wanted to say he had spoken of his wife and had reconciled with his God. But all she could remember was eyes still angry.

And that he had asked for Rob.

'They cared for him,' she began, meaning to reassure. 'At the end. He…'

And then neither of them could speak for the tears.

'And did they care for you, child?'

There was an edge to the question. How much could her mother see? And how could she even begin to explain what had happened over the last weeks?

'Yes,' she said, finally. 'They did.' To say another word would be to admit all.

'But—'

'Go. Rest. We'll talk later.'

And her mother withdrew with her husband's body and her grief.

Behind Stella, the rustle of men. She turned to see that Rob had been surrounded by Storwicks, held tight as by a living cage. Her eyes met his, but she could not let hers linger.

'He is here because your head man asked him to come,' she said, as the men escorted him out of her reach. 'He must come to no harm.'

'That does not mean we must leave him free to roam and spy.' Humphrey's voice grated on her ear as she looked up to see him walk down the stairs from the wall. He was one of the Red Storwicks that Stella had claimed to be, red-haired and blue-eyed with skin so fair it chapped in the summer wind.

Oswyn, younger, smaller, and darker, came after.

'I have brought my father home,' she said, as they came closer. 'We will give him the burial he wanted.'

Or the one her mother did. The priests would come. They, too, would look at her, waiting the way that Humphrey and Oswyn waited now, standing just a foot too far away.

'So,' Oswyn said, clearing his throat. 'Did you do a miracle, then, while you were gone?'

She started to shake her head, to say no, to face his disappointment and her own. Then, she smiled instead. 'Aye,' she answered. 'I brought my father home.'

He looked at her, sceptical. 'How is that a miracle?'

How could she explain how many small guided, steps it had taken to get here? Even those she had once thought misguided, like her first headstrong move across the border. Somehow, step by step, day by day, she had crept closer, too close, she had thought, to Rob Brunson. Close enough that he took her to Carwell, so she could see her father before he died. Close enough that her father asked to be brought home.

And that Rob had said yes.

She smiled, thinking of God's mysteries, and motioned her head towards Rob, surrounded by Storwicks in the courtyard's corner. 'You see that man?'

Humphrey looked over his shoulder. 'Aye. What of him?'

'That's Black Rob Brunson.' The name rolled off her tongue, delicious, for she knew the taste of the man, as well as the legend.

'You tell me nothing I don't know,' Humphrey said.

Oswyn swallowed, silent, and nodded, his eyes shifting from Rob back to her.

'He is here because of Hobbes Storwick's last request. Here because he honoured the dying wishes of his sworn enemy. Here to pay his respects before a fellow warrior is laid to rest.' Her heart swelled with the words. All these things he had done for her, yes, she knew that, but also because he honoured her father. 'A Brunson paying respects at a Storwick funeral. I can think of no greater miracle than that.'

* * *

The Bishop of Glasgow may have severed the men of the Borders from the church, but this family, Rob saw, still clung to theirs. Hobbes's wife insisted a priest be sent for, so Rob was forced to wait until one could be brought.

In the meantime, he found himself an unwelcome guest of the Storwick family. 'Guest', in this case, meant that he was a prisoner instead of a dead man. They treated him much as he had treated Stella at the beginning. He was given a room, one even finer than his own, boasting not only a curtained bed, but a tapestry on the wall. But the room came with a guard at the door and no opportunity to roam at will.

And no moment alone with Stella.

Better that way. He must break the habit of her.

He saw her only in the Hall, at meals. He was isolated. Put at the end of the table, served, but not spoken to. And she, it seemed, had near the same treatment.

The mother had retired to her room in grief, so Stella sat alone at the high table. No one else laughed with her, or spoke to her in passing or of small things. She had wept, he could tell that, and it hurt his heart.

Bessie had looked just so, after their father had died.

But no one else seemed to notice or care. No one came forwards to comfort her. No one took her hand or put an arm around her shoulder. Neither adult nor child came close enough that her hem might touch a boot. Even the serving girl stood out of reach, as if afraid to enter some invisible halo surrounding her.

They simply watched her, and left her alone.

All my life, people looked at me. Watching. Waiting. Expecting me to do something worth being saved for.

That had bound them. He could see that now. As she grew, no one had been willing to touch her. As he grew, everyone had given him a wide berth. Respect. Fear. Awe. It didn't matter what you called it, the effect was the same.

A life alone.

And for those few times, those few nights together, neither of them had been alone. Now, forced to stand apart from her, he ached for the one person unafraid to touch him.

One night, he had said. One would have to last for all the ones to come. But though his body pined for her, it was his heart that had suffered the mortal wound. Who else was willing to challenge him as she did? Who else was willing to tease and argue and love what he had done while asking for just a little more?

Who else would demand fish and then help build the trap to catch them?

She had asked him to stay and he had said yes. Not because he respected Hobbes Storwick, though now that he was head of the clan, he had more sympathy for the man.

No, he stayed because he was not ready to let her go.

And he must. There was no other answer. King James would ride in a matter of weeks, mayhap days. And when he did, Stella Storwick must be safely on her side of the border.

Yet the thought made him feel as if his heart were being ripped from his chest.

Stella had forgotten how scarce priests were on the Borders. It took her cousins till week's end to find one who could bury her father and even then, the mass he read was a ragged thing.

They held the service in what had once been a chapel for the tower. Stacks of hay, ready for re-thatching the charred roofs, had to be moved to make room.

Stella did not recognise the priest. He carried a sword, his garb was as tattered as a battle flag, and when she got close enough to kneel for his blessing, she caught a whiff of wine on his breath.

Even so, she was surprised he did not know of her. When she was a child, men of God had visited regularly, watching her, like the rest, as if she might sprout wings at any moment. Someone had spoken of certifying the miracle with the Church, but she did not know what had come of that. It had been many years since the monks had named her saved by God.

Perhaps only the Storwicks remembered now.

The consecrated burial ground was not far away, beside a church long abandoned. She watched the men lower her father into the grave. Then, holding her mother's arm, she turned to leave.

'Is there no one to sing for him?' Rob was suddenly at her elbow, tall, quiet and full of strength. Still, she could tell the church ritual had made him uneasy.

'Sing for him?'

'Do you not sing to honour the dead? Do you not create a new verse to hand down his name?'

Her mother shook her head. 'There is no one left to do it.'

He looked over his shoulder at the grave, fast being filled. 'He did not die as a warrior should, but he deserves to be honoured.'

Stella glanced at her mother, expecting her to protest. Instead, she waved a hand, too weary or grief-stricken to care. 'Do as you like. He is gone now.'

Leaving them, Rob returned to the grave. The men with shovels raised them, wary, as if they thought Rob might have come to piss on it. Instead, he gazed into the dirt for long minutes.

Her mother did not wait. With a murderous look behind, Humphrey moved to flank her right, Oswyn her left, and they walked back to the tower.

Unmoving, Stella watched, neither joining her family nor Rob, but unable to leave him.

Finally he began to sing.

The tune was new. The verses few. Rob could have chanted of mayhem and destruction wreaked upon innocent Brunsons. Instead, he sang of a man of courage, beloved by his family, in a voice so deep and in words so true that the men filling the grave leaned on their shovels and bowed their heads.

And as the final notes floated into the hills, she heard the words with a shudder.

And what will be his legacy?
What mark upon the hills?
When Hobbes Storwick lies in his grave
Who will remember still?

No one left, her mother had said. Without her father, what would happen? Of all the care he had taken, all the things he had done for the Storwicks, he had never trained a successor. Without a son, without a marriage for Stella, there had been no obvious heir.

Rob turned to look at her, the question of the

song lingering in his eyes as if she might have the answer. Instead, her tears came again, tears for Hobbes Storwick and for the future.

She waited until he had come to her before she tried to form the words.

'Thank you.' Just two words and her eyes filled again. Her father dead. And a Brunson the one who seemed to mourn him most.

He answered only with a shrug and open hands.

As one, they turned towards the castle. She longed to curl into his chest, to feel his arm around her shoulders, to take comfort in his closeness. Instead, they walked a safe distance apart, afraid of even an accidental touch.

'Is it near?' Rob's voice, still close. 'The well where it happened?'

Stella's steps slowed. She had told him, of course, but they had never spoken of it since. 'Near enough.' She knew exactly where it was, the better to avoid it.

He folded his arms, a gesture that on another man would have been threatening. Instead, she felt he was holding himself back from touching her. 'Would you show me?'

She looked away and folded her own arms, shielding herself from the fear. 'I never go there. Someone else draws water.' Someone else had done everything for her in this life. Its own kind of prison.

'It's nay more than a hole in the ground, Stella. You spent the night with worse.'

She smiled. 'With you?' Yet she knew his meaning.

'Sometimes, we must face the fear.'

Perhaps, with him beside her, finally, she might. But what came after, losing him...ah, that was a fear she would face alone.

'Come.' She turned away from the tower walls.

Rob hesitated. 'It is outside the walls?'

A tower under siege would need water. A good leader would know that.

She nodded. 'That is why no one heard me.' She pointed up the hill. 'It's up there. In one of the old forts.'

Together, they turned towards the hills. No one followed them.

In truth, Stella was not certain she could find it again. Oh, she knew where the old walls were. All of them did. But to deliberately walk up to that hole in the ground and stare into the darkness...

No. She had never had the courage to do that.

Yet now, with Rob at her side, she found her way by instinct. Bluebells beckoned her on, a trail to follow.

You used to love the hills.

Aye, she could imagine that on a day such as this, wandering into the hills when she was little more than a babe, too young to know fear...

The momentary joy evaporated. Her muscles tensed. Ah, her body remembered. They must be close now.

The old fort where the early ones had lived was worn smooth now. Only indentations in the grass showed where mighty walls had stood, yet some sloped high enough that she could gaze over the valley.

There. In a corner surrounded by weeds. She knew it. And could not take another step.

Rob came closer and gripped her hand. They had not touched since entering the gate for fear the madness would seize them again, but his hand was a comfort now.

'Here,' she said, still not moving. 'It is here.'

And she felt the breeze in her hair and the sunshine of June on her cheeks and cringed.

The well had been dark and cold.

'It's no more than a hole in the ground,' he said, his voice rough in her ear. He nudged her back in encouragement.

She crept forwards, as if she must catch it unawares, as if it were a live thing, only sleeping, and ready to roar to life if she woke it.

A few more steps.

Even from here, she could not see the well itself. Grasses and ferns sprouted around it, hiding it. It would be easy to miss, easy for a child to run right to it and tumble in, with never a chance to hesitate—

She squeezed his fingers.

'Just a few more steps, Stella. I won't let you fall.'

She took them, pausing, finally, a few inches from the edge. The wind rippled her skirt over the yawning blackness. The earth seemed to tilt beneath her.

She dropped to her knees, never letting go of his hand, feeling safer closer to the ground, held fast by the earth. And as she peered over the side, she saw only stones.

She leaned closer. Where was the shaft, plummeting deep into the earth? Where was the water, waiting to swallow her? All that was here now was gravel, close enough to touch.

She looked up at Rob, seeing safety in his brown eyes, and tried to catch a memory...

'I don't understand. It was deep and dark with water waiting at the bottom. This is...' She waved her hand, ashamed. 'Harmless.'

He wrapped his arms around her, rocking her against his chest, but she would not be comforted. 'Was I wrong? Were they all wrong? All this time?'

'Who knows? The wall might have crumbled in since then or they might have deliberately filled it to save the next child.'

Explanations all logical. But shame bit her still. She had been afraid...of what? A story her mother had told her?

And if it was only a story, then why?

The shame ebbed and she could breathe again. Breathe as she had not for fifteen years.

She would fear the well no more.

Chapter Sixteen

Each step Rob took towards Storwick Castle dragged.

This last day he had spent with her had only prolonged his agony and postponed the inevitable. It was time to mount Felloun and ride home across the hills, thanking God he was done with Storwicks.

The hollow longing for her had become as familiar as a wound.

Beside him, Stella walked across the grass with a smile. Of course she would smile. She was home and free of the fear that had haunted her all her life.

She needed him no more.

As for Rob, he had honoured his enemy's wish and returned his body home. His father would not have done it, he was sure, but he was head man now. The decision had been his.

Yet poor Hobbes Storwick must be in Purgatory grumbling at the poor stewardship he had left behind. Money spent on tapestries, while roofs stayed unthatched.

Grateful again, Rob thought of his father and the hours he had spent at his elbow, learning what a head man must. Duty. Courage. Strength. The doubts that had plagued him ebbed. The Brunson clan was in good hands. His.

Humphrey and Oswyn spent more hours squabbling with each other than planning for battle or even for daily life. Even their sheep staggered under coats of unsheared wool.

No wonder they had not ridden to save their head man. These two fools could not agree on what to have for dinner.

Wat Gregor had more sense. And more integrity, too, he'd wager. Neither would step aside, yet neither was strong enough to assume leadership of the other, or the rest of the family. So the world slowly crumbled in their wake, until the family would be no threat to anyone else.

And no bulwark against them, either.

Stella might smile now, but he could see the future, as if he had the sight. One day, if not in this generation, then the next, the Robsons or the Elliots or some other family from either side of the border would swoop down and discover the Storwicks were defenceless and the family would be no more.

He should have relished the thought. He didn't.

But if he had learned anything these last days, it was that his father had been wise to choose and groom his successor so early.

And that Rob needed to do the same.

If something happened to him tomorrow, Johnnie could, would, step in. But if he were to protect the family for the next generation and the next, it was his duty to marry, beget sons and train them. There had been a First Brunson. There must not be a Last.

He knew his duty. Yet when he looked at Stella, wild longing gripped him. He wanted to grab her, mount Felloun, race across the border and hold her for ever.

A selfish dream. A violation of his duty and her happiness.

He had kept his word to her father and brought

her home. They had been reluctant to ransom her, true, but now he had witnessed the reverence in which they held her. He was certain they would let no harm come to her, no matter what danger the rest of the family might face.

But the price of that reverence, the lonely, isolated life she would lead here, twisted his heart.

A sense of peace settled around Stella as they left the hill. She had bidden farewell to her father and laid him to rest and with him, thanks to Rob, she had laid to rest the fear that had haunted her her whole life. For those few moments, to be Stella, walking beside Rob in the sunshine, seemed enough for all the world.

Yet her calm disappeared as they approached the gate.

What had happened all those years ago? Why couldn't she remember? And what parts of her mother's story were true?

'I'll be leaving, then,' he said, next to her.

A shadow, fear, returned. Aye, there was what she had tried to forget. She would have to face those questions alone. 'It's late. The day's near gone. Wait until tomorrow.'

Just a little longer...

She reached for his hand, as if that would be enough to change his mind.

He pulled away the instant her fingers met his. 'Don't make it harder.'

She had reached for one more day, one more hour, as if she could extend their time together. As if she could run away with him, disappear, and make time stand still until a miracle happened and they were allowed to be together.

But miracles were scarce on the Borders and it seemed she had reached her limit.

'It could not be any harder,' she said, her voice dull with defeat.

He did not turn away from her gaze and she saw in his eyes that his agony equalled hers. 'Aye, it could.' Grim words. 'You could be with child.'

Without thinking, she touched her belly. It was too soon to know whether his seed had taken root. Surely God would not be that cruel.

Or kind.

She looked away, to hide her tears. Looked to the hills and the path he would ride home. She knew, now, what was on the other side. A valley that would no longer welcome her.

'Tell Wat,' she began, struggling with the words, 'that I did not abandon him. Tell him…' She cleared her throat. 'Tell him that I love him.'

I'll love you all my days.

But for Rob duty would always come first. As it should.

They entered the courtyard, not touching, and he went directly to the stables. She trailed behind, as silent as he, for nothing she could say would change the fact that she was a Storwick and he a Brunson.

But when he mounted Felloun and gathered the reins, he looked down at her. The darkness on his brow, she saw now, the reason they had called him Black, no longer seemed the darkness of anger, but of sorrow.

He cleared his throat. 'If you ever need…' The sentence died in his throat.

She shook her head and looked away. If she met his eyes now, neither one would have the strength to fight desire.

The horse walked across the courtyard, slowly, it seemed, as if he, too, were reluctant. No one approached them and the gate swung open, no impediment to his departure.

Outside, Rob kicked Felloun into a gallop and she watched him until horse and rider were swallowed by the hills.

He did not look back.

That evening, Stella took her place at the high table, alone with her grief and her questions. Her mother had taken to her bed and no one else dared come close.

Except Humphrey Storwick.

Throughout the day, he had paced, agitated, but never approached her. She'd been glad of it, though her skin ached for Rob's. More than that, her soul missed the only one unafraid to be near her.

Humphrey leaned closer, trying to be close enough to whisper, but not succeeding. 'Would you speak with me in private?'

Something to do with the running of the house, she supposed, though she had never been asked to do so before. But she had learned some things at the Brunson Tower. It would be better to come down from her pedestal and to keep busy.

In the corridor, Humphrey stopped, abruptly, but backed away when she did not halt quickly enough to keep her distance. He swallowed and licked his lips. 'I must marry you tomorrow.'

'Must?' The word seemed even more objectionable than *tomorrow*.

'Yes. If I'm to be head of the Storwicks.'

She shook her head. All those days, all those years she had longed for someone to ask for her hand, for intimacy, for children. Now, it was too late.

Not because she had given her virginity away, but because she had given it to Rob. After him, everyone else would be no more substantial than a feather in the wind.

Yet, a fleeting question. What would happen if she was with child?

No. Even that would not force her to wed this man, so inadequate to rearing Rob Brunson's babe.

'You don't need to marry me,' she said. Humphrey's eyes, wide, seemed to hold more fear than admiration. 'The family will reward the man best suited, no matter who his wife is, or even whether he has one.'

'But I need you.'

'Need me?' There was no passion in the word. None of the yearning so deep it could not be spoken. 'I hear nothing of love in your voice.'

'Love?' He looked at her as if she were daft. 'I said nothing of love. I need you because marriage to you will prove God intends me to lead. After we are wed, do as you like.' He shrugged, not meeting her eyes. 'Go off to work more miracles.'

Alone, he might as well have said. *Take care of other people's children. Walk around untouchable, as you have done all your life. Just make me the head man.*

'You're strong enough to lead the Storwicks or you're not.' There had been no question, she was certain, who would rule when Geordie Brunson died. 'Marrying me won't make it so.'

'Say what you like,' he said, furrowing his forehead in an expression meant to be menacing. 'It will happen. Before the priest leaves on the morrow.'

Behind her, Oswyn's voice interrupted. 'Or me. You can marry me.'

'No, she can't. She's going to marry me.'

'Not if she doesn't want to. Let her choose. That's why God saved her. To choose which of us will lead.'

God, she was certain, had saved her for nothing of the sort. 'I'll live in a convent before I marry either one of you.'

'Your mother will see reason,' Oswyn said, turning to leave the Hall. 'I'll ask her.'

Humphrey followed, arguing to Oswyn's back.

A chill touched Stella's shoulders. Her mother must know the real story of what had happened to her that day. If Stella confronted her, what would her mother say?

Possibilities began to swirl. Had Stella fallen down the well, or had she merely disappeared for hours, as Wat might, unmindful of what her parents thought? Perhaps she had simply wandered too far from home and been frightened when she found herself alone?

Yet her fear of the well, that place, was real. Something had happened there. What? If it was not a miracle, if she had not been saved by an angel, then who had saved her?

* * *

Stella's mother summoned her before the first star showed in the gloaming.

A summons from her mother had always unsettled her. When Stella was a child, it had meant lessons or a lecture in a room that seemed always in perpetual twilight.

Not this time, she promised herself. She had questions of her own to ask.

She entered silently, as she had been taught, and waited to be recognised. At least today, the dark shadows were appropriate to mourning.

Her mother knelt at her prayer stool, the place she had spent so many hours during all of Stella's life.

I'll live in a convent. That's what she had just threatened, knowing it would be a sacrifice to give up the world.

She wondered, not for the first time, whether her mother might have been more suited to that life. And for the first time, she wondered what her father must have thought of it. Now that she knew what could happen between men and women, she saw with different eyes.

Her mother struggled to rise and Stella went to

her side, offering an arm. Her mother patted her hand. 'God was good to us when He sent you.'

The burden of the day, of her husband's death, had sapped her. Her eyes drooped, her shoulders slumped, her very skin sagged, as if too tired to cling to her frame, and she leaned against Stella for the few steps between the prayer bench and her chair.

Stella helped her sink into the seat and then waited, silent, no longer certain she could challenge this woman whose piety had shaped her whole life. Not now, when she had lost so much.

Her mother's head rested against the high-backed chair, her eyes closed. 'God answered only one of my prayers,' she said, finally, never moving her head. 'He sent you home to me.'

'Yes, Mother.' No need to ask what prayer went unanswered when her father lay mouldering in his grave.

Strength seemed to flow into her mother again. She lifted her head and opened her eyes. 'The man is a poor excuse for a priest, but he is the one God sent, so he is the one who will marry you.'

Stella swallowed a scream. 'Who would you have me marry?'

'Humphrey. Oswyn. The choice is yours.'

'I choose neither.' She wanted to say more. Wanted to say that a man who could not make himself head of the family without her approval would never be able to make the difficult decisions a head man would be forced to make. Like disowning Willie Storwick.

'But you must.' Her mother tilted her head, puzzled.

'Why?'

'Why else would God have sent you back to us?'

No other reason. Not that she was loved or wanted or seen as anything other than God's instrument.

There is nothing special about you, Stella Storwick. But to Rob Brunson, there had been, and it had nothing in it of reverence, but of relish, of appreciation of her body and her heart. And the rightness she had felt with him seemed more in tune with her purpose than the feigned honour her family accorded her.

'It was not God who brought me back. It was Black Rob Brunson.'

'That,' her mother said, with a nod, 'is a miracle only God could have performed.'

'I visited the well today, Mother.'

Her mother blinked, like a startled bird. 'Why? You've not been there in the years since God saved you.'

'I had to face it.' Rob had understood. Why hadn't her parents? Why had they let her drag the dread with her for all these years? 'And do you know what I found there?' She paced now, looking at her mother and away, gathering energy. It was as if everything in her life had been upended. 'I found a gravel pit no deeper than my arm.'

Her mother looked away. 'We filled it, later. We filled it in so it could harm no one else.'

She paused. Rob had suggested the same, but nothing seemed true now. There was nothing she could trust. There had been fear—oh, yes, fear her body still carried. But was it the fear of the trauma she could not remember? Or the fear she would never live up to their expectations?

'What really happened, Mother?'

'It will do you no good to relive this, child. You screamed for days after. I couldn't comfort you.'

She ignored the regret on her mother's face. 'How long was I gone? An hour? Two? It wasn't days, was it?'

'Hours seem like days to the mother of a lost child.'

She bit her lip, knowing the truth of that. Hadn't she felt the same for those minutes Wat had been missing?

'But I searched for you,' her mother said, in the words Stella could recite from memory. 'All day and all night and then, after I had looked everywhere in vain, I went to the chapel and lay on the floor praying to the Virgin, a night and a day, more...'

Praying while a little girl waited, alone and in a dark well.

'Did they search for me while you prayed? Father? The others?' There was an answer somewhere. One she had missed all these years.

Her mother waved her hand. 'It matters not. It was the Virgin who saved you.'

Stella sighed. If there were truth beneath the tale, it seemed to have been lost long ago. 'So the Virgin told you where I was?'

Her mother nodded, smiling now. 'She gave

me a vision and I went to the well and there you were, in the arms of an angel.'

The same words, the same story. 'If you knew I was in the well, why did you go alone? Why didn't you take someone with you to help get me out?'

'The vision was clear. The angel had saved you.'

'What if there had been no angel? What if you had been wrong?'

What if God had decided I didn't deserve a miracle?

'The vision was clear. I was to go alone. Now come, child.' She stretched out her arms. 'We have both suffered these past weeks. We must ask for God's guidance again to lead you in the right path.'

And she reached for her mother's outstretched arms, knelt beside her and buried her head in her lap.

She had come home. Home to the confusion, expectations and isolation that had dogged her all her life. And now, to questions she had never asked before.

In contrast, life at Brunson Tower seemed

simple. Caring for Wat. Catching a fish. Simple things that connected her to the earth and to other people.

But in coming home, she felt lost again.

She raised her head, cheeks damp with tears she did not remember shedding. 'Tell me the story of the Lost Storwick, Mother.'

And so she listened to her favourite tale of the woman isolated and alone, who defied all their expectations and escaped.

'What do you think happened, Mother?' she asked, when the tale was through. 'To the Lost Storwick?'

Shaking her head, her mother smoothed Stella's hair and wiped her tears away. 'No one knows. Some say God took her. Others say it was Satan. And a few think she escaped on her own two legs and wandered into the hills where she met another lost soul and married him.'

Wandered into the hills, just as she had done. And met another lost soul. One like Rob Brunson, perhaps.

But Rob was never lost when it came to his family. He had never doubted his duty, nor questioned what he must do as she was doing.

She sighed and pulled herself away. Standing, she brushed her skirt and scrubbed cheeks with the back of her hand. Duty, that's what Rob would say. Miracle or no, this was her duty.

'If God saved me to select the next head of the family, that's what I will do.' She would not fear that. No more than she feared a pit full of gravel. 'But I will do it in my own time and in my own way.'

Perhaps God could deliver another miracle. There was someone, anyone, more worthy than these two.

Yet as she left the room, she wished that, like the Lost Storwick, she could simply disappear.

Chapter Seventeen

Rob had regretted leaving her before the stone walls of the Storwicks had disappeared behind him.

There was nothing else to do. She was with her people. Safe.

Blood was all. Family was all. Generations of Brunsons knew that. No Storwick's fate could be more important than his duty.

Why did he doubt it now?

And as he rode through the gate to Brunson Tower, he told himself anew that he had done what he must, what was needful, what was best for them both.

Until he saw Wat, running up to him, eyes full of hero worship. And then he saw that Rob was alone.

'Where is she? Why didn't she come back?'

He did not wait for answers, but screamed and howled as if he knew without being told that Stella would come no more.

Rob dismounted into a flurry of kicks and fists, as if Wat thought he could punish Rob for his own sorrow. Rob let them bounce off and scooped the boy into his arms, rocking him as if he were a baby still and could be comforted simply by being held.

He put his forehead close to Wat's and whispered, as he knew she would want him to do, 'She told me to tell you she loved you.'

If only she had told me the same.

His brother, when he settled to talk, looked little more content than Wat.

'You took her home, then.' Johnnie's expression seemed too knowing.

'With her father's corpse.' Rob tried to sound appropriately gruff, but the vision of Hobbes Storwick, laid in the ground unsung, made him shiver.

'Cate liked her.'

'Are you sure?'

There was the smile. 'She's me wife. I'm sure.'

'And why do you tell me this?'

'She would not have minded. If you had brought her back with you.'

Too late. Too late to fill that gaping hole where his heart had beat a few weeks ago. 'She was no good to us once he was dead.' In truth, it seemed they had never needed protection against the Storwicks. Once Hobbes Storwick was gone, they were helpless. 'One less crime for the King's list.'

'What will happen to her, do you think?'

He frowned. His brother's question was the very one he did not want to consider. 'It's nothing to me.'

A lie. Yet he must make it true.

Johnnie sipped his ale and stretched his legs under the table. 'She'll marry, I suppose.'

There was Johnnie, needling around the edges, smiling without saying exactly what he meant. But the spectre of Stella in another man's bed was more than he could bear.

Gritting his teeth, Rob put down his mug and stood. 'Well, so must I. It must be the Elliot lass, then. A wedding and an alliance before the King rides will give extra strength to the Elliots who ride with us.'

And end this lunatic moping over a woman he could never have.

After only a few days at home, Stella was ready to run to the hills again.

Once, her family had given her respectful, though lonely, distance. Now, not an hour went by without Humphrey or Oswyn or her mother approaching her expectantly. Sometimes, they asked about the defences of the Brunson Tower. More often, they questioned her about her current intentions.

No one was waiting for God's miracle now. They had decided what it was to be, and instead of blessing it she was standing in the way.

Yet the longer she watched the household, the more she was convinced that to marry either man would mean the end of the Storwick family.

She had seen how the Brunson Tower was run and though she had chafed at the lack of luxuries, it seemed that now, that was all she saw. Decadent food and sumptuous fabric covering crumbling walls and dull swords. Mundane necessities, repairs, defence, all languished. Even the weir that Rob destroyed had not been rebuilt. Ashamed, now, to think how she had chided him, when protecting his flock, human and animal, was always his first concern.

Would that the Storwick family had a leader as strong as Rob Brunson.

Aye, that would take a miracle.

Or, maybe, something else…

I'll marry someone special, she had said, when he taunted her. And then, ignorant and naïve, she had decided her sacrifice was to marry him. Before she knew all that loving entailed. Before she knew they were flame and tinder.

Before she knew that Rob would let nothing dissuade him from his duty. Even Stella Storwick.

'Stella?'

She looked up, startled to see her mother, Humphrey and Oswyn standing together. Uneasy, she looked from one to the other. 'Yes?'

'It seems, daughter, that you have been unable to hear God's guidance for you amidst the noise of daily life.'

'You can't even remember how many men defend the Brunson Tower,' Humphrey added.

'I told you I was a prisoner.' She licked her lips, praying God to forgive her lie. 'They did not allow me to roam freely, no more than you let Black Rob do.'

'We've been patient long enough. You must choose or—'

'Your mind has been clouded,' her mother said. 'We must take you somewhere quiet where you can hear His voice.'

'Perhaps I should retire to the chapel until the Virgin sends me a vision.' Bitter words. Words she'd never thought, let alone spoken aloud.

Her mother gasped, as if she'd been slapped.

'We've some place better in mind,' Oswyn said.

And his fingers dug into her arm, deep enough to bruise, as he dragged her away.

The King must be on his way.
That was Rob's first thought when the messenger arrived to let him know Thomas Carwell would be arriving before sundown.

His brother-in-law always announced his coming, the better to prevent Rob from shooting him off his horse before he reached the gate.

Still, sometimes his finger still quivered on his laich.

But this time, he recognised Bessie's flaming hair beside the man and found himself wishing that there was fish in the larder.

'Is it the King?' he asked, before Bessie could even dismount to hug him.

She looked at her husband, leaving him to answer.

'Not yet.'

Cate and Johnnie rushed out and there was a flurry of greetings.

'Then what brings you?' They had not ridden for two days because the weather was fine.

Bessie looked down and then at him. 'We've heard something. About Stella.'

The pit of his stomach dropped and he swallowed, wondering why his ears seemed to be ringing. Too late to pretend he did not care. They knew better or they would not have come.

'When I left her, she was home. Safe.' That was why he had left her. So she would be protected by her kin.

Next to him, Cate put her hand in Johnnie's. 'No one is ever safe surrounded by Storwicks.'

She said it as if Stella were a Brunson, too.

Johnnie glanced at him, but spoke to Thomas. 'Why would you have heard anything of the Storwicks?'

'I am still Warden of the March,' Carwell said. 'The English Warden and I exchange…information.'

'Can you trust his?' Rob growled. He resented Carwell's closeness to the English Warden, though he was grudgingly grateful at this moment.

'Hear it first,' Thomas said. 'Then decide. He tells me the family has barricaded Stella in a sheiling hut until she agrees to marry.'

'Marry?' As if he had not known she must. 'Until she agrees to marry who?'

Thomas raised one eyebrow, the gesture of a man who knew too much of hidden motives. 'Either Humphrey or Oswyn Storwick. Whichever she, or God, chooses.'

'That's no choice at all! They are bigger idiots than Wat Gregor!' *Nothing but weaklings left.*

'No doubt. But the burden is hers to choose

one of them. And the one she marries will be leader of the Storwicks.'

Why would the Virgin save me? To choose the next Storwick head man, apparently. And he would marry for the power and the position. Not because he loved a stubborn, headstrong woman who was afraid of the dark. No, the only special thing about her to that man would be her position. The only thing most women had ever seen in him.

The four of them, Bessie and Thomas, Johnnie and Cate, even Cate's beast Belde, stood in a tightening arc, looking at him. Watching. Waiting.

'What are you looking at?' Jaw tight. Muscles coiled. 'What do you want me to do?' He knew what he wanted to do. If he let himself go for one minute, he would be on Felloun and riding for the hills.

His father would have killed Rob himself before he allowed his son to sacrifice his family to save a Storwick.

The others exchanged looks, but it was Cate who spoke. Cate who had suffered more at the hands of the Storwicks than any of them. 'Go after her. She shouldn't be forced to wed. No woman should.'

Could Cate mean it?

He looked at his brother, who nodded. *She would not have minded,* Johnnie had said, *if you had brought her home with you.*

'It's a Storwick family matter. None of ours.'

'It's not the rest of the family we're worried about,' Bessie said. 'Only Stella.'

Had they all gone mad? Was he the only one who knew what a Brunson's duty must be? He battled temptation with another argument. 'Why should we trust the English Warden? He's betrayed us to the Storwicks before.'

Thomas frowned at the reminder. 'He told me because I asked.'

And why had Thomas Carwell cared? Had the man become as womanish as the rest of them? 'Well, Lord Acre won't take kindly to my kidnapping her. And neither will the King.' As if the King's opinion had ever held him back.

Thomas smiled and took Bessie's hand.

'If we had feared the King's opinion, we would not have come at all.'

If they had feared the King's opinion, they would not be wed.

No. He was the one his father had trusted to hold the clan together. He had been chosen because, unlike Johnnie and Bessie, he put the family above any weakness he might have for a certain dark-haired, green-eyed Storwick wench. It was selfish to even consider his own happiness.

And yet, as he saw them, each united with a loving partner, they seemed to have found something that had eluded him. Contentment. Peace. Happiness.

Love.

Weaknesses he had avoided. Things he had never been selfish enough to want. Things he had never believed he deserved.

Before...

And neither had Stella. Both of them chosen by their parents for some higher purpose more important than personal sentiment. Well, he did not know what Stella's purpose was, but he was certain it did not involve marriage to Oswyn Storwick.

They all looked at him, expectant. Cate nudged

the dog forwards. The dog who had found Stella one long, dark night not too long ago. 'Bring her home, Rob.'

All the tightness seemed to leave his body. And he knew what he must do. What her father, God rest his soul, would want. He nodded. 'I'll not let her be shackled to one of those weaklings.'

What consequences would he spark? Well, he would consider those when they came.

There was no well hole in the middle of the dark, dank sheepherder's hut where they took her, but Stella choked on her fear even so.

Her mother had pressed a crucifix and rosary into her hands as Humphrey and Oswyn stood out of earshot.

'God will guide you,' her mother said, with a grip tight enough to crack her fingers. 'We are waiting.'

Stella looked down at the boxwood beads draped across her clawed hands and felt nothing.

They put some food on the floor and closed the door on her. The roof sloped low and steep.

The stone walls were barely tall enough to stand and the holes to let light in were small.

In prosperous times, a shepherd would be sleeping here only during the few, dark hours of summer. Otherwise, he would be out with the sheep.

And when she heard them drop a bar across the door, she could barely stifle the scream.

And then she was grateful for the beads, for they allowed her to pray to God, not for guidance, but for deliverance.

Rob's first instinct was to storm the Storwicks' stronghold. He had seen enough of the layout to know where they could enter and had seen enough of the Storwick fighting men to know that, without Hobbes, they had become soft and lax.

But he was not willing to put his men at risk for his personal desires. No. Once again, only the closest of family would do. He and Johnnie and Thomas Carwell would do this alone.

They, to taunt the Storwick men and cause a diversion.

And Rob? Rob would find Stella.

* * *

Stella had lost track of the days.

Outside the sliver between the stones, light came and went. Once a day—or was it every two days?—someone opened the door and came with food. When it opened, the light almost blinded her.

Once, her mother had come to pray outside her door. 'Has God sent you any visions, Stella?'

She laughed at that one. Aye, God had sent her visions. Of Rob Brunson. Of being in his arms, of taking him inside her.

In fact, she was sure now. He was inside her still.

No woman's time had come to her since her father's death. The babe she had always wanted was growing inside her. And when, if, they ever let her out, she did not think they would believe that God had visited her like the Virgin. The child would be in danger if her sin were discovered.

Yet what could be a bigger miracle than a babe made between the heads of Brunson and Storwick? What could be a larger purpose than to bring peace?

The old thought, of marrying Rob, took root amid the dark days, clinging like a plant that clutched a stone.

Was it from God? From the delusions of loneliness? Logic? Or just a stubborn heart? She wasn't sure. But it comforted her in the dark hours.

If only she could sneak away and cross the border as she had done before. But she could not be certain Rob would have her. Certainly Cate and Bessie would not. And Rob would never choose her over his family.

And so, another day passed. And another night.

Rob followed Belde into the hills as the sun disappeared. The June night was short. He had not much time.

Her scent still clung, faint, to the handkerchief, thankfully not destroyed by his own. Belde had caught it and Rob took him back to the place they had crossed the border and picked up her trail from there. If he was lucky, the dog would catch the fresher scent from the direction her family had taken her.

If not, he might end up squarely in front of the castle, in a perfect position for Storwick target practice.

Fortunately, Belde veered higher into the hills, tracking a small stream as if it had been her footpath, leading him into pastureland that should have sheltered a flock. But if Storwick sheep were grazing in the hills, it was on another slope.

Belde quickened his pace. Seeing by starlight, Rob could make out three huts, normally sleeping quarters for the shepherds. The dog ran immediately to the centre one, sniffing around the door, tail wagging, impatient for Rob to rejoice in the success of the hunt.

Rob dismounted slowly. No guards. No light. No sound. Nothing to indicate anyone was within.

Until he came close to the door and saw it barred from the outside.

Fury propelled his arms. He pulled off the board, near ripping the brackets away as well, and opened the door.

At first, Stella thought the noise part of her dream. Then, when a man loomed over her in the dark, fear gripped her for an instant.

Sadness replaced it when she recognised the curve of the muscles on his arms and the familiar scent of leather and the earth of his valley.

I have conjured him in my dreams.

And then she squeezed her eyes, not wanting to wake.

Belde's cold nose and rough tongue brought her to full alert. Not dreaming. Awake.

And Rob, real.

He kneeled and reached for her face, reading it with his fingers. 'Did they hurt you?'

She opened her mouth, but her throat, unused for speech in days, remained stubbornly silent. Instead, she shook her head, knowing his hand would feel the motion.

No, they had not hurt her. Not in the way he meant.

A sigh. Relieved. 'I don't want to leave you here,' he said. 'You're not safe as long as they want something you have.'

She smiled and touched his hand. 'And I'll be safe with you?'

He shook his head. 'I'll guard you with my life.'

'And safe from you?'

He sighed. 'Aye. That, too.'

She smiled, as if she knew what he meant and did not say. The minute she signalled she wanted him, neither of them would be safe.

'I won't force you, lass, but I'll take you away from them, if you want to come.'

'What if they come for me?' Hard to know what Humphrey and Oswyn would do. They had done nothing before, but the stakes were higher now. And if she put Rob in danger...

His fingers tangled in her hair, as if trying to read her. 'We Brunsons are a tough lot. Besides, your kin won't know where you are.'

She felt herself relax into a smile. 'I'll just disappear like the Lost Storwick, eh?'

'Until you are ready to be found. For as long as you want.'

And if it is for ever? But she could not ask that. Not now. The babe, tomorrow, all an uncertain mystery. But she must decide, not knowing.

She cleared her throat. 'I'll go.'

'You're sure?'

'Yes.' Louder this time.

She was scooped into his arms and the rosary slipped to the floor. And when he carried her out into the starlit night, it seemed like blazing noon compared to the darkness in which she had lived.

Chapter Eighteen

When they entered the gate of Brunson Tower, at dawn, Stella sat before him on the horse, much as she had the first day he had captured her on the hill.

No one moved at first. The stares, the distance, all the same, whether at home or here. Whether because she was honoured or the enemy, no one would come close.

Except this man, whose chest pressed against her back, strong and safe.

As he helped her down from the horse, a small, blond bundle hurtled towards her, squeezed her somewhere around the knees and pressed his head against her belly.

She wrapped her hands around the boy's head and held him close, smiling.

'You came back.' Wat's words were muffled in her skirt. 'He told me. He told me you loved me.'

She looked up, lips parted, eyes wide. 'You said that?'

Rob shrugged. 'The lad was having fits.'

Did he know she had meant the words for him, as well?

Wat lifted his head, grabbed her hand, and tugged her towards the gate. 'I put the sticks back. We can catch fish again. Come see.'

Something twisted in her chest. She had inflicted her pain on him. 'That's good, Wat. I've been hungry for fish.'

She looked to Rob for permission just as Cate and Bessie entered the courtyard. Belde loped over to Cate, sniffing her in greeting, while Cate looked to the gate and then to Rob.

'They'll be back soon,' he said.

'Johnnie?' Stella asked, astonished. 'And Thomas?'

'Inspecting Storwick sheep to see if they are worth borrowing,' he said.

She bit her lip and met Cate's eyes and then Bessie's. They had risked their husbands. For her.

And though she was sure that stubborn Rob

would have acted alone, to think his family had supported him, supported her, made her blink back the tears. Had her own family ever done so much?

Bessie stepped forwards, briskly. 'Come, Wat. Give her time to rest.' She smiled at Stella, even though her words were for Wat. 'She's had a long journey.'

'Did you…?' She did not know how to ask. Why were Bessie and Thomas here? Fresh air and freedom had revived her brain and for the first time, she wondered how Rob had known she needed his help. 'What…?'

'Take her upstairs, Cate,' Bessie said, with the brisk efficiency Stella remembered. 'I'll take care of the beast and the boy.'

Silent and uncertain, Stella followed Cate back up the now-familiar stairs, astounded to find herself back in her old room.

'I can't stay here.' There were only two private rooms. The head man's and this one.

'Where did you think we would put you? Down with the well?'

'But you and Johnnie, Bessie and Thomas…' If she was here, the others would have no privacy.

'Just for tonight,' Cate said. 'You've had a hard time of it.'

At that, Stella cried.

Oh, she had cried before. Tears had been too close a friend. But this was different. This time, she cried all the tears she had hoarded since before memory. Tears of fear for those dark, lost hours. Tears of joy at being rescued. Tears of frustration for having a life thrust upon her, owned by everyone except Stella Storwick. And tears because she had finally, if only briefly, found a man who swept away the loneliness.

And she cried because this Brunson woman, who had all the reasons in the world to hate her, had been kind.

Cate let her. She did not flutter, or cluck and hug, or pat her shoulder and take her hand. Cate simply stood, silent witness to her fears, honouring her grief.

The wave passed near as quick as it had come and Stella brushed her cheeks dry.

'It never fully leaves you, the fear,' Cate said, calmly as if she knew everything. 'But when you take control of your own life, it ebbs.'

'How…how can you know?'

'Because I let a Storwick control my life for too long.'

Kind thoughts, but for Cate, 'Storwick' had been an enemy. Fear of a foe was to be expected. Overcoming it, a mark of honour.

But Stella feared her own family and that could blight her life as fully as her terror of a cold, damp well. Their blood ran through her veins, and yet, they had treated her as cruelly as a hated enemy.

Why?

A wish danced through her head. *Stay away, wander the hills, never return to face them.*

But that happened only in long-ago legends. Thanks to Rob, she had disappeared as completely and mysteriously as the Lost Storwick, but that was only a reprieve. Questions, mysteries, remained.

She must find the answers.

Thomas and Johnnie were home by midday, full of smiles that faded when they saw Rob's face.

'This came,' he said, holding up a message.

It carried the royal seal.

Wordless, the three men gathered in the private chamber. Rob handed the letter to Thomas, a man more accustomed to reading. Thomas opened the parchment, holding it up to the window to catch the light.

Yet Rob knew what it meant, even before Carwell spoke.

'The King rides the Borders to hunt for sport.'

'To hunt for Brunsons, you mean,' Rob said.

Thomas's smile was rueful. 'No doubt. He must prove to his uncle King Henry that he can keep order on the Scots side of the line. Otherwise, according to the cursed treaty, the English have the right to come into the valley and enforce it themselves.'

Johnnie frowned. 'He'll not be happy to find you've a Storwick captive.'

'She's nay captive. She's here of her own free will.' True it might be, but her people would never believe it. Nor would the King.

'He'll be here within the week,' Thomas said, an edge of warning in his voice. 'With eight thousand men.'

'I'll fight him.' His hands, of their own volition, fisted in futile fury.

'With how many men, Rob?' Johnnie knew the answer.

Rob let his fists fall. Brunson and Carwell and Elliot together would not be half so many. Fighting was all he knew, but it might not be best for his people. Not this time.

And he was weary of warring.

'There must be a way,' Johnnie said, 'to make peace with him. Some of the Border lords have promised to give good governance. The King agreed—'

'The others didn't have warrants with their names on them,' Thomas said sharply.

Rob felt a moment's regret. Thomas had flouted the King's orders. Now, his fate would be that of the Brunsons. Because of love.

And who was he to say it had not been worth the trade?

He rose. 'He also writes that he comes in peace. I'll nay call the King a liar. Let him come and promise him our hospitality on the word of a Brunson. Then we'll see.'

Rob walked out into the sunshine, the weight of all the generations since the First on his shoulders, wondering what Geordie Brunson would have done.

Confront the King's force? Disappear into the hills where the King would never find him? Or harry the monarch's men, just to prove he could?

This time, it would not be Geordie Brunson's decision. It would be his son's.

Since his father had died, every step had been nothing but doubts. His father had been taciturn. Even more so than he. Geordie had never said, 'Yes, you are doing it right.' Rob didn't get constant praise. He didn't know whether he was pleasing his father or not.

Occasionally, maybe once a year, the old man would look at him and smile. And nod. That was all.

He had always hoped that some day, his father would clap a hand on his shoulder and say, *Yes. Now. Now you are ready.*

And every time they had gone on a raid, he had braced himself. Would it be this time? Would he be the one left alive to lead the men home?

But his father had died in his sleep in his own bed. One morning, Rob woke up and it was all on his shoulders. No equals. No peers.

And then Johnnie had come home, challenging everything his father had stood for. What was a man to do then? Who was right? His father? His brother? Rob wanted his brother by his side. Instead, they had spent months in a private war until Johnnie realised that he, too, was a Brunson.

Next, his sister had defied him to marry Carwell, a man he was ready to kill for treachery. Family was supposed to trust you. Obey the head man. Did they not because he was doing it wrong?

Who saved him? Stella's question niggled at him. He brushed it aside. A man like the First Brunson didn't need someone else to save him.

But Rob Brunson? He was beginning to think he did.

Johnnie joined him, silent. Together, they climbed the steps up to the wall walk and faced east, knowing the valley would be shaking with the King's horses within days.

'After all this time, I thought I was ready,' Rob said, glad of his brother's ear. 'I thought he had taught me everything I needed to know.'

'He couldn't,' Johnnie said. 'No one could.'

No, no one could have taught him what to do about a certain Storwick woman. Or, if they had, the lesson would have been this: *Cut her out of your life.*

He could as easily cut out his heart.

Instead, he had told her he loved her. And never, in all the time since, had she said the same.

What was he to do now?

Arguments, opinions, he must listen to them all, but in the end, the decision would be his. No one else to blame if he made the wrong one.

He looked towards the hills that sheltered them. 'At least you know something beyond this valley. You were the one he chose for the privilege of seeing the world.' All those years his brother had spent at the King's side. All those years Rob had missed him.

Johnnie looked at him, wide-eyed, then laughed. 'I was the one who was banished. You were his true son. The one he wanted with him.'

'The one he didn't trust to be out of his sight.'

Johnnie stifled a grin. 'You know what Bessie told me, once? She said he sent me to court because I needed to be away from here in order to become my own man. He must have thought you were strong enough to become yourself despite him.'

'What if he was wrong, Johnnie?'

What if I am wrong now?

'Well, if he was, he wouldn't be the first.'

No. Even a head man was not perfect. Hobbes Storwick hadn't been.

Johnnie's hand gripped his shoulder. 'But since you ask, no, he wasn't right about everything. He wasn't right to create you in his own image, but he was right to choose you.'

He grasped for the comfort. 'And yet you've fought me every step of the way.'

'What's a brother for?' Said with Johnnie's familiar, easy smile.

Something Rob had never mastered. 'Support.'

His brother's blue eyes turned serious. 'Hear me. Whatever you decide, about the King, or about Stella, I'll be beside you.'

Strong enough to become yourself. Not just Brunson, but his own man, too. That was a different kind of fight.

It would take a new kind of courage.

Courage to face Stella Storwick.

For one decision at least could not be solely his.

* * *

Late in the afternoon, Stella was surprised to hear Rob's knock.

'Come,' he said, when she opened the door. 'I must show you something.'

They rode into the hills in silence, in a direction she had not travelled before. And all the way she argued with herself, summoning her courage.

You will be alone together, finally. You must tell him about the babe. You must tell him you love him, tell him you want to stay.

And never go home again.

Then, as they came over a rise, she saw the stones, laid in a circle on the slope, and slowed the horse. 'What is this place?'

'This is where I come from. Hogback Hill.'

She shivered. She had heard of the place, but never seen it. Or wanted to. Spirits lived there. Spirits of Brunsons past. Spirits, she was sure, ready to kill a Storwick.

He helped her off the horse and she stood a safe distance, not wanting to cross some imaginary line between her and the stones. The summer day stretched as long as the shadows cast by the stones. They were not tall. No higher than her waist, with strange symbols on sides that curved to a peak.

Refusing to cross into the circle, she stroked the patterned stone, then pulled back her fingers, quickly. 'This one looks like a fish, all the scales even.'

'Some say they are houses for the dead,' Rob said. 'I like to think this is where the First Brunson lies.'

No Christian, then, she thought, squinting at the symbols. A bloodthirsty pagan Viking like the ones who had crushed her ancestors.

'Under which stone?'

He shrugged. 'No one knows.'

'And the woman?' The one he loved.

'Aye. I think she's here, too.' He looked away. 'But someone else lies here, too. And you should know.'

He held out a hand and she took it. He led her around the edge of the circle, to a ravine that yawned a few feet beyond. There, the hill dropped sharply to a stream, too far away to hear. The slope, interrupted by outcropped stones, slanted at an unstoppable angle. All she could hear was the wind, as if it filled the hole.

She gripped Rob's hand more tightly. One step over the edge and a body would keep going until, bruised and bleeding, it landed at the bottom.

'He's down there,' Rob said. 'Scarred Willie.'

Where's his body? she had asked Cate. *At the bottom of a ravine, where it belongs.*

And she felt a strange mixture of relief and regret. 'Did Cate kill him?'

'Cate and Johnnie and the dog and Scarred Willie were all up here. Willie didn't come down. They've never said more than that.' He smiled and she saw the pride in it. 'Though the ballads tell their own tales.'

Tales of spirits, no doubt. She looked around, wondering whether they watched her, a Storwick, waiting. 'I'd like to hear them some time.' One evening, sitting by their own fire.

His smile faded and he was Black Rob again. 'Stella, the King is coming.'

'Which king?' They had not even a king in common.

'The Scottish one. And he's none too pleased with me.'

She slipped a hand in his. 'Then he doesn't know you as I do.' The heat in her breasts and between her legs reminded her how well she knew him.

And how long it had been.

'Stella, I told them, the others, that you were here of your own free will.'

She nodded, thinking there was something more.

'Is it true?'

She smiled, the ease in her body a testament to the truth of it. 'Yes, Rob Brunson, it's true.' *Now, the time to tell him is now*—

'And when you are ready to leave, you must say so.'

You can stay as long as you want, he had said.

He had not said for ever.

Now, her nod was numb. She had thought to tell him for ever when he expected, even wanted her to leave.

The King will be here soon.

And when he found Stella Storwick, things would not go easy for Rob Brunson. Was that why he had wanted to know?

'Do you want me to leave now, Rob?'

He looked away, hiding his eyes from her while his tongue, as reluctant as hers, gave a silent answer.

I shall love you all my days.

But never had he asked her to share them. He had said the words after a night of passion, just before returning her to her family. Said them when he was sure he would never see her again.

She looked back down into the gash in the earth, deep and wide as that separating her family and his. She felt closer to Rob than to anyone with her own name, but she knew that it was only in bed that they could pretend there was no Storwick, no Brunson.

Everywhere else, they were enemies.

How could she have thought that would change?

'If you'd let me, I would stay a little longer,' she said, grateful she had kept her silence. No good to speak of love that could never see sunlight. No good for him to know of a child whose blood he'd despise. Better that he brought her to this spot and warned her before she confessed it all.

Yet she could not go back to a home where

nothing, not even her past, was certain. Perhaps she *was* destined to roam the hills as the Lost Storwick did, at home on neither side of the border.

'Just…' she stumbled over the words '…a little longer.'

'How long, lass? How long?'

She swallowed, speechless.

Without another word, they turned back to the horses.

Chapter Nineteen

When they returned, Stella saw the tower brimming with activity. The courtyard was being raked, the tower scrubbed, pots were clanging in the kitchen.

The King will be here soon.

A royal visitor. Of course, there would be much to do.

Rob had been tugged away as soon as they entered and she caught a glimpse of Bessie, directing Beggy Tait with an ease Stella had never felt.

She stood, letting the work swirl around her. Well, the least she could do would be to help.

But first, she would be sure her chamber was empty and ready for a visitor. More of those three thousand men the Brunsons could raise had arrived. She would sleep in a corner of the corridor, if necessary.

She had virtually nothing to collect, she realised, as she looked around the room. Even her rosary had slipped away when Rob had brought her here. She had nothing of the Storwicks but the clothes that covered her skin and the cross around her neck.

A rustle of skirts and she turned to see Bessie at the door.

'I was clearing the room,' she said. 'In case it is needed. How else can I help?'

Relief edged Bessie's smile. 'A hand with the washing would not be amiss.'

Working in silence, they stripped the bed-clothes. 'When does the King come?' she asked, finally.

'A week. Maybe less.'

'And he'll be housed here?' She could not envision it. The tower was strong, but not fit for a king.

'We do not know what will happen.'

The King is not happy with me.

And then she realised. Food stocks, sharp weapons, all prepared the tower for an attack or a siege as well as for guests. And she'd be trapped here, in a war that was not hers.

Do you want me to go? Rob had not said yes. But he had offered her a chance to escape.

'You, Cate, all of you have been more kind than I had any right to expect.' In fact, virtually nothing about the Brunsons had been as she had expected. 'I am grateful.'

'He's my brother.'

Simple words. But the implication warmed her. *Because I care for him and he cares for you.* Was that what Bessie meant?

Yet the caring, even the loving, wasn't enough.

Stella carried her small bundle, borrowed comb and chipped looking glass, to the top floor and tucked them in an out-of-the-way corner. In the corridor, Thomas Carwell suddenly appeared, windblown from the parapet, frowning.

She stepped back. She had exchanged few words with the other men of Rob's family, particularly this one. But his frown seemed specifically for her and she raised her chin, determined to address it. 'Is there something you would say to me, Lord Carwell?'

His eyes narrowed. 'Rob tells me you have chosen to stay.'

She nodded. 'For a while.'

'Do not let the King see you. Not if you care for him at all.'

He turned away and went down the stairs.

Suddenly, it was all clear. The King would assume she was a captive, no matter if she argued otherwise. And though it was not true today, it had been true, once. That, on top of what was no doubt a multitude of other sins, would be enough to hang him.

But did she love him enough to leave him?

And could she leave him knowing she carried his child?

As if her thoughts had conjured him, Rob appeared before her. She tried to read his face now, to understand what lay behind his eyes, but all the softness she had glimpsed was gone.

He was Black Rob again. And a Brunson.

'Come.'

Rob clenched his hands to keep from touching her as he led her to a corner of the parapet out of sight of the man on guard.

A little longer, she had begged. Just as she had tried to hold him at the Storwick Tower. Which of them was the weaker? She for asking, or he for agreeing?

Well, he must be the strong one now.

And the bravest thing he did was to look into her eyes when he spoke.

'I took you home.' Like cutting out his heart, but a decision he had made with his head. 'Thinking your kin would keep you safe.'

Her eyes darkened. No, not safe. With scars he had yet to discover, scars that might never heal.

Once more, words he had said to her too often. 'I'm sorry.'

She shook her head. 'You could not know. I thought it was for the best, too.'

'But when I learned...' The next decision, for good or ill, had been made from the heart. Now, he must keep the anger at bay, along with the love. 'About what they did, I came to take you back.'

Had that been a better choice? It had put them in limbo, that place at the edge of Hell reserved for unbaptised infants, not together, yet no longer enemies.

'And I thank you.' She reached towards him, but he stepped back.

He must not touch her. Not if he was to finish.

She sighed. 'And that has brought fresh danger, for you this time.'

'You are not safe with your family.'

'And I put you in greater danger here.'

Relieved, he watched her look away, giving each of them a moment to think.

'There is only one place I can think of to go.' She looked back at him. 'Will you take me?'

A few days later, astride a sturdy Brunson pony, Stella watched the red stone abbey glowing hellish in the reflected sunset. Around her, the horses galloped much too quickly. She was almost there.

Rob had brought a small group of men. Enough for protection and enough so that they had not a private moment.

And what would she have said to him if they had?

He held up a hand to stop the group, still far enough from the walls that an arrow could not reach them. Even God's houses were ready to defend themselves on the Borders.

'You'll be safe here,' he said.

She nodded.

'We'll stay until we see you inside.'

He had taken risk enough, to bring her back over the border. Not home, but to this small abbey, where a few holy brothers and sisters still prayed for the salvation of men's wicked souls. Where she would be safe, at least, from the worst that Storwicks could do to her. And he would be safe from the crime of holding her.

A little longer, for ever, both were no more. Her gaze clung to his and she searched for a word that was not *farewell.*

'You're a good man, Rob,' she said, finally. 'Even if you be a Brunson. I'll be praying…' She would not cry. 'I'll be praying that the King spares you and yours.'

He nodded, never a man generous with thanks. 'God be with you.'

Did she hear tears in the words?

She turned her horse towards the abbey's gate and heard the other horses retreat as she entered the courtyard.

A white-robed monk greeted her. She gave him her name, too weary to say more.

His eyes widened. 'Stella, daughter of Hobbes? Your mother has just arrived. She did not tell us you were coming.'

She was not given a choice, but was ushered immediately to her mother's room.

Her mother knelt on her prayer bench, smaller and more frail than only a few weeks ago.

She rose, her back to the door, not knowing who came, but when she turned to see Stella, she dropped back to her knees, eyes wide. 'Another miracle. God saves you again. We went to the hut, the stone was rolled away, as if you might have risen.'

'You put me in that place, that awful place.' Anger nearly throttled her words. 'How could you?'

'I thought, we thought...' Her mother looked around the room, as if expecting the angel to appear. 'It was time. Time for you to find your reason. The reason you were saved. And then, God performed another miracle and you were gone—'

'There was no miracle, Mother!'

'Blasphemy! Of course there was. The hut was empty—'

'No. There was not.' This time, she would make her mother hear. 'There was only a Brunson who came to save a Storwick.'

At the simple statement her mother's face froze. Shaking fingers formed the sign of the cross. 'God did not forgive me. All the prayers and still He holds me to account.'

An answer, at long last. 'For what, Mother? God holds you to account for what?'

She shook her head, tears speaking what words could not.

'There was no miracle all those years ago, was there?'

Fear, shame, guilt, relief—what were the emotions flickering across her mother's face?

'Tell me the truth, Mother. What really happened?'

A lifetime of lies, finally, not strong enough.

'The fault was mine.' Her mother's words, muttered like a prayer for forgiveness. 'All mine. I did not watch you as I should have. You wandered off, disappeared...'

She could feel the fear, even taste it. Had she

not suffered the same way when Wat was lost? Regret, guilt, thinking *if only...*

'I was young and tired and careless and I fell asleep. I didn't even know when you had gone.'

Forty days and forty nights. For ever. All the same to a fearful mother.

'What happened then?' She had to creep up on the story, cautiously as she had approached the hole in the ground, for the truth of this would be deeper and still dangerous.

'I had to find you, but I couldn't ask for help. Everyone would have known then what I had done, how bad I was. So I went alone.'

'Did I even fall down a well?'

'Oh, yes. That's where I found you. I lay on the ground and tried to reach you, but you were too far away. You cried, oh, how you cried, and I was crying, but I couldn't reach you and God was going to snatch you away from me because I had been a bad mother.'

Long-buried pain played over her face, fresh as if she lived it still. And then, beatific peace smoothed it all away. 'That's when he appeared.'

'Mother! There was no angel!'

'No, not an angel.' Her mother faced her now. 'A Brunson. A Brunson saved you.'

At the words, Stella's very skin seemed to lie differently over her bones.

A brown-eyed angel. No wonder her mother had not wanted her to remember. 'What Brunson?'

'I don't know which one, I never saw him again, but I knew those eyes and the way he carried his spear. He was a Brunson, all right. He must have heard me crying. All of a sudden, he was just there, tall and strong enough to reach down and pull you up and place you into my arms.'

No reason for a Brunson to ride alone on Storwick land in daylight. Or perhaps no more than for a Storwick to cross the border looking for her father.

'So you told a different story.' One that would hide her guilt and the Brunson's goodness.

'And I've spent the years since praying for forgiveness.' Her mother nodded, not meeting Stella's eyes.

All those days and nights on her knees, and still… 'But did you confess? To a priest?'

Penance, absolution. Such were the church's blessings.

'How could I? Even your father never knew.'

Stella saw it all now. The years had passed, and the longer her mother stayed silent, the greater her sin. By avoiding the confession of this, her most grievous act, she now stood in danger of being cast from the church altogether.

Then, as if admitting the truth, finally, had released her, she grabbed her daughter's hands, all eagerness again. 'You see, don't you? If an angel saved you, if God answered my prayers, then no one would blame me for letting you wander away. It would all be part of God's special plan for you. But to admit that my neglect had put you into a Brunson's hands…' She shook her head. 'No. That I could never do.'

Stella turned her head, unable to meet her mother's eyes. Instead, she looked around the small, barren room, as unfamiliar as the truth she had just learned. No miracle, then. Or not the one she had been taught. Just a small child wandering too far from home, lucky to have the help of a kind stranger who just happened to be an enemy.

No expectations. No reason God had saved her. Just Stella, an ordinary woman, free to follow her own destiny.

Free.

Once, she had believed that the miracle gave her power. Now, she could see it had made her powerless. She had been at the mercy of everything her mother or her family or the priests or her own fears had made of it, her life wasted, waiting for God to tell her what to do. She would wait no more.

She would make her own miracles.

She rose and placed her hand on her mother's bowed head, and bent to kiss her head. Benediction. Forgiveness.

And turned to leave.

Her mother scrambled to her feet and grabbed Stella's hand. 'Where are you going?'

'Twice now, I've been saved by a Brunson. That's a debt that wants repaying.'

'You won't tell them. Please, don't tell them.'

Her mother was still trapped by the truth. She was not. 'Tell them? Tell them what?'

'That God did not save you.'

'Did He not?' She smiled. 'Who is to say,

Mother, that an angel might not come to earth disguised as a Brunson?'

Her smile came with her as she left the room to cross the border once again.

She had little more of a plan than before. And this time, she would *need* a miracle.

Rob felt the earth shake before he heard the hoofbeats. Coming from the east at a gallop, still too distant to make out the colours, but he did not need to see the banner clear.

King James had come at last.

No talk, no conversations among them now. They had decided what to do and each man moved into his position: his second-in-command atop the tower, the other above the gate. The men stretched out around the tower, clear that they were there to defend and not attack.

Cate and Bessie stayed inside the walls, though Cate had grumbled at it until Johnnie reminded her that Bessie was with child.

And Stella… He pushed the unwelcome thought away. She was safe. It was done. Better, perhaps. He might be a dead man by day's end. Rob mounted Felloun, surprised to see Johnnie and Thomas flank him as he rode towards the gate.

'I do this alone,' Rob said. 'If something happens, I need you here.'

'Save your breath, Brother,' Johnnie said.

'Johnnie and I know the man. You've never dealt with him. Do you think we would let you go alone?'

He started to argue, then realised it would be futile. And as they rode out together, he felt surrounded by a shield stronger than any armour.

Below the King's castle, so Bessie had told him, stretched a field near as large as the valley where men dressed in armour and sword and fought each other for fun. And died anyway.

If the King chose to make this a battlefield, he was ready to die, but not to sacrifice the rest of the Brunsons. They could defend the tower, if need be, for a long, long time.

Rob pulled his horse to a stop close enough to shout at the King. For a few moments, they all sat, silent. No man smiled.

Rob was the only one of them who had never seen the King. Tall, red haired, and still sporting the gangly limbs of a boy, the King rode a destrier, decked in horse furniture as fancy as French armour.

Shifting his gaze from the King, Rob assessed the men around him. Dressed for hunting game or men, the garb was the same. And the numbers? Not eight thousand, then, but enough.

He looked to Johnnie and Thomas, and they nodded. He urged Felloun one step forwards. 'I am Rob Brunson. Welcome to my valley,' Rob began.

'It's not your valley,' the King snapped. 'It is mine. I rule here as surely as I rule the rest of Scotland.'

You cannot rule soil you've never even seen. This land belongs to the Brunsons and has since the First.

At Johnnie's warning look, he forced his unruly tongue to silence.

The King did not wait for an answer. 'Thomas Carwell, Warden of the March, for the last time, will you bring me this outlaw?'

'And what charge would you have me make of him?' Carwell, beside him, called back.

'There are so many to choose from,' Rob muttered.

'First, he disobeyed my summons to bring men to war against my enemy.'

'Ah,' Thomas said, 'a misunderstanding. He was defending Scotland's border here. So his men were still riding in your service.'

'Not where I had asked him to be,' the King answered.

'But where your Grace would have sent him had you known the threat here.'

The King scowled.

'Why doesn't he punish you?' Rob muttered to Thomas. 'You've disobeyed his orders near as often as I.'

'He may still. But last time someone other than a Carwell was Warden of the March,' Carwell said, 'chaos ensued.'

The King's voice echoed again across the field. 'Carwell, since you have been too busy to call a Truce Day, as the treaty requires, I have done it.' He looked to the south and waved his hand.

The herald beside him raised a long hagbut and fired into the air.

As if they had been waiting for his signal, a new army rode out of the hills.

Beside him, Carwell spat a curse. 'It's Lord Acre.'

And the English Warden was followed by every Storwick who could mount a horse.

They halted, equidistant from the King's men and the Brunsons.

'Now,' the King began again. 'I come to enforce the laws.'

'If this is to be a Truce Day, then we must put aside the weapons,' Carwell called out.

No one made a move to lay down arms.

'And I come,' the English warden said, 'with a warrant for Rob Brunson, head of the clan.'

'What are the charges?'

'The unlawful killing of Willie Storwick.'

Carwell exchanged a glance with Johnnie. 'It would have been a lawful killing if he had not been snatched away from Truce Day justice.'

'Does he not want our heads for the raiding or the burning?' Johnnie said to the two men beside him. 'Or for taking their head man captive?'

'Storwicks have done the same. Too bad this killing was the one even Hobbes Storwick forgave.'

'So, Rob Brunson,' Acre continued. 'Either

surrender, or give us the man responsible for the killing of Willie Storwick.'

Johnnie smiled and gathered his reins. 'Tell Cate I love her.'

Rob held up an arm to stop him.

Suddenly, from high on the tower's wall, came Cate's voice, clear and proud. 'Then you'll have to take me. I killed Willie Storwick.'

Johnnie looked up at his wife, fear and anger mixed on his face. Then, he turned back to the King. '*I* killed Willie Storwick,' he roared.

'Nay. *I* killed Willie Storwick.' His sister's voice.

Beside him, Carwell shook his head in disgust, but he added his voice, unwilling to let his wife stand alone. ''Twas none of them. I killed Willie Storwick.'

And then, the air was crowded with confessions. One by one, the men lining the barmkin wall joined their voices, glad to claim they had killed a man who deserved to die. Even Belde howled in chorus.

And then, as the voices died down and quiet took the valley again, Rob could hear a horse approach from behind and he heard the last and most surprising voice of all.

'It was none of them,' it called out, loud and clear. ''Twas *I*, Stella Storwick, who killed Scarred Willie.'

Chapter Twenty

Stella saw Rob's shoulders stiffen with shock before he twisted in his saddle to stare as she rode up to stand her horse between him and Thomas Carwell.

She knew Carwell to be a man who seldom spoke an unconsidered word. She hoped he wouldn't find one too soon, for if he tried to save her, everything she was trying to do would be for naught.

And Rob? Well, she'd glimpsed unguarded joy on his face. His grin was warring with the angry frown of frustration that she'd not stayed safely where he put her.

Well, he would become accustomed to that.

When she had left the Abbey, she'd no more of a plan than the day she'd come to spy, but

God seemed to have delivered her just in time. Her sudden appearance and her confession had struck both sides dumb. The English Warden put his head together with her Storwick cousins, who were staring and pointing as if they had seen someone raised from the dead.

And then, she looked to the King.

He looked perplexed, but not the way her cousins did. He looked as if he knew exactly what she had done and was now trying to work out his best response.

Even a hot-tempered king of Scotland who would summarily hang a reiver would think twice before doing the same to her. She might have confessed to a killing, but she was a woman and an English subject who had killed another English subject. King Henry would not take kindly to King James's interference.

'You see,' she called out, now that she had their attention, 'it was Black Rob Brunson who discovered the truth of it.' She risked a glance, then. One that warned him. ''Tis why I sit before you a captive.'

'She did not kill him!' Oswyn near sputtered

with frustration. 'I killed him! Punish me instead!'

'You didn't kill him,' Humphrey countered, apparently unwilling to let Oswyn lay down his life to save Stella's. 'I killed him!'

She choked back a happy laugh. On either side of her, Rob and Thomas disguised smiles. Humphrey and Oswyn had opened their mouths once too often.

Now Rob lifted his voice. 'So you claim she lies?'

The cousins' jaws sagged. Murderer or liar, they could not call her either and expect a marriage to elevate them to lead the family.

Besides, they both had just confessed to murder.

Even from this distance, she could see the King would have gladly murdered the lot of them. She had stopped him from a quick execution of Rob Brunson, but something else would have to stop him now. 'As you can see, your Grace,' she called out, 'even his family members are proud to take credit for his death.'

'And if they killed him,' Carwell chimed in,

having reclaimed his voice, 'Lord Acre has been complicit for refusing to punish…someone.'

The King's face had turned as red as his hair. She could see the man would be dangerous. He had not yet learned to temper his emotions with his mind.

Rob spoke, finally, his voice clear and calm. 'But it seems that if your Grace plans to punish a murderer, you'd better know for certain which man, or woman, actually did it.'

He should be furious with her, Rob told himself. And he would be. Later. As soon as he stopped smiling. Her presence spoke as loudly as the words he'd waited to hear: For ever.

Aye, mayhap she had been saved for a miracle. For if they all escaped this moment unscathed, that would surely qualify.

Johnnie and Thomas whispered across him, trying to come up with soothing words that would make the King back down.

He let them talk. He would be the one to make this decision.

Not long ago, he would have asked himself

two questions first. *What would my father do?* and *What will make me look strong?*

The answer would like as not be: *Attack.* So he would have charged ahead, relying on his strong arm and his crossbow to conquer any foe, even if he be king.

But blunt force, he had learned, was not the answer to every problem. Not to Stella. Not even to little Wat.

And it was not the only sign of strength.

After all, a man needed a little peace if he was to start a family and raise a son.

'It seems, then,' he said, finally, 'that I should continue to hold her until this is resolved.'

'You can't do that!' Which one of her cousins said that? Of no more consequence than the squeak of a titling bird.

'Well,' Rob answered, 'since you've confessed, I could hang you instead.'

At that, they fell silent.

Thomas spoke up, the words of a diplomat. 'As you know, your Grace, Scarred Willie Storwick had been banished from his family. He was a man known for committing wicked acts on both

sides of the border. It is possible that God punished him without waiting for earthly justice.'

'He won't believe that,' Johnnie muttered
under his breath. 'No more than you did when
we told you the same story.'

'Certainly,' Rob called, loud enough so all
could hear, 'if both Storwicks and Brunsons are
happy to claim the honour of killing the man,
his death is no loss to mankind.'

The King frowned, as petulant as Wat when
he did not get his way. 'Even if you and yours
did not kill the man, I'm sure there are men you
have killed.'

'Only in self-defence.'

'That has a broad meaning on the border,' the
King snarled.

Rob waited, holding his breath. Silence could
be a weapon now.

Finally, the King spoke again. 'Will you promise me, Rob Brunson, will you give me your
word to obey the Border Laws?'

'I will give you my word to live in peace with
the Storwicks,' he said. 'If they will promise the
same.'

Lord Acre and the Storwick cousins huddled in whispers.

Rob tensed, waiting. The soft clop of horses and he realised Bessie and Cate had ridden out to join them. 'I told you to stay safe within the walls.'

Did no one heed his orders?

But with Bessie beside her husband and Cate beside hers, he saw the rightness of it. And wished he could take Stella's hand.

Finally, Lord Acre faced them. 'The Storwicks agree.'

The King turned back to Rob. 'And in the future, will you answer my summons?'

Aye, he would serve the King's interests. Just not in the way the man expected.

'Your Grace, as long as there are Brunsons in Liddesdale, we will defend the land from any who would cross the border to take it.' His warning was clear. He would keep the peace with the Storwicks. As long as they kept the peace with him. 'So you need not worry, King James, that your uncle, or any of the English, will steal an inch of Scottish soil.'

But answer the man's summons to fight in

some strange Scottish valley as if he were a dog called to herd sheep?

No.

Even at this distance, he could see the King shake his head. Refusal? Resignation? Or the reaching of a hard decision?

Stella was beside him. Johnnie and Thomas flanked them on either side, with Cate, fierce Cate, just to Johnnie's left. And Bessie, showing her state once a man knew where to look, Bessie, on the other side of Thomas, was giving the King a stern look.

One king against six Brunsons? Truly, Rob felt sorry for the man.

Then, King James raised his voice and looked to Johnnie, the man who had been like an older brother to him.

'You told me, Johnnie Brunson, that you came from stubborn stock. And you, Bessie Brunson, you told me that when a Brunson had a choice to make, he asked only what would be best for the family.' He sighed. 'A king must think of all Scotland as his family. And Scotland is composed of many families. A king must balance the needs of all of them.'

He brought his gaze back to Rob.

Well, now it comes. Whether I've done good or ill.

He looked at Stella and, in the smile they shared, he knew if the King decided to kill him, he would die happy.

'But any king,' King James continued, 'would be fortunate indeed to have such a bulwark on his border.'

He did not repeat his requirement that Brunsons answer his summons, which showed him Rob's outright refusal.

'I think,' Thomas whispered, 'that means he will let you keep your head.'

Rob growled, a vain attempt to hide a smile. 'Then I'll let him do the same.'

The King gathered his reins and looked to the lords who rode with him. 'So, Carwell, as my Warden of the March, can you work with this Brunson man?'

Rob watched Carwell, whose face revealed nothing. The man had disobeyed the King's direct orders. Yet James was offering him the chance to stay in his service. 'Yes, your Grace.

And on the Borders, a Warden who can work with the Brunsons will ultimately do you well.'

'Well, I won't!' The English Warden's howl echoed across the field. 'Your Warden was the one who violated the Truce Day you promised England in your treaty.'

Carwell's expression was grim. Rob did not know all that had passed between those two men, but he knew each had been guilty of betrayal. 'You're not one to speak of violations of Truce Day, Acre.'

But the man was not to be stopped. 'Instead of carrying out the king's justice, he and these rogue raiders snatched Hobbes Storwick away and our head man is now dead at their hands! They have killed more than one Storwick.'

'Not true!' Stella's voice floated from beside him. 'My father died of the wasting sickness. And he died regretting there was no one trustworthy left to lead the family.'

A quarrel broke out among the English and even the King's men started talking and pointing, each pressing the King to listen to his opinion.

'Maybe you should not have listened to me,

Rob.' Carwell's smile was rueful. 'Maybe we should have kept the Truce Day.'

Rob shook his head. He had not truly trusted the man then, but now? Yes. Carwell was a Brunson, too. 'If we had gone, we would have been ambushed and ended up at the end of a rope.'

'We still may.' Johnnie nodded towards the King. 'I know that look. He's not a happy man.'

King James waved the rest to quiet. 'Johnnie Brunson. Ride to meet me over there.' He pointed to a clump of grass in the middle of the valley. 'Alone. Just you and me.'

This was how it had all begun, months ago. Johnnie had come home bearing the King's orders. Rob had refused them. And Johnnie had gone from being the King's best friend to being a mortal enemy. 'Don't do it, Johnnie.'

His brother, still, always, smiling. 'I'll be all right. Just don't shoot the King.'

Rob gripped his crossbow. 'Only if I must.'

He watched his brother ride to the centre of the empty space and stroked the trigger of his crossbow.

'Careful of your finger.' Carwell's voice was tight.

'I'll be as careful as the King with his dagger.'

He watched them speak a few words. Both tall, lean, red-haired. Then the King clasped Johnnie's hand and his arm. A brother's gesture. And one of farewell.

The King rode to his men and Johnnie came back to them.

'Well?' When had his brother's face ever been so unreadable?

The King exchanged a few words with his men.

Suddenly, Acre was surrounded.

'Come with me to Edinburgh, Lord Acre,' they could hear the King say. 'Enjoy my hospitality. And I'll enjoy telling my uncle, King Henry, that you were the one who let Willie Storwick ride free instead of trying him as justice demanded.'

Acre paled, frightened into silence.

'King Henry is not going to like that,' Rob said, quietly.

Bessie's husband grinned. 'A flurry of diplomatic letters will ensue.'

Unusual. Carwell never let his feelings show. His history with Acre must go back a long way.

Rob allowed himself a moment's regret. The English Warden had, after all, been the one who had let them know that Stella was in danger. For that, he hoped the man might keep his head.

The King threw one last look, and a wave, to Johnnie, and turned his men to the east.

'We were like brothers, once,' Johnnie said, watching him go. Then, he turned a smile on Rob. 'But I've my real brother now.'

'Don't celebrate too soon,' Rob said, warmed by his words. 'We're still facing a brace of armed Storwicks.'

And with the King gone, there was no buffer between them.

'I wouldn't worry,' Stella said. 'They'll dither for hours over there, I vow, discussing whether they should attack.'

Indeed, the shouting and pointing, the babbling and arguing had commenced. Surrounded by his family, Rob had never felt stronger.

Johnnie's familiar grin returned. 'The Storwicks need a new head man. Anyone can see that.'

'Someone strong and stubborn,' Bessie said.

'Someone who can keep the peace,' Carwell said.

'And keep a king in check,' Johnnie said.

'Someone who marries a Storwick would do,' Cate said.

'Although the King would want to give his approval,' Johnnie reminded him.

'It's forbidden to marry across the border,' Carwell said.

Enough of his family telling him what to do. Even if it was exactly what he wanted. 'No king will choose *my* wife.' He had agreed to defend the border against invasion. Nothing more.

Beside him, Stella beamed. He wanted her to look as happy every day of the rest of her life.

'Brunson and Storwick,' he said. Names still difficult to join. 'Enough of a miracle for you, my love?'

'The one I was saved for.' And then she cupped her belly. 'That, and your child.'

Only long practice prevented him from whooping with joy. But his family had stood with him through all. 'The rest of you?' He looked to Thomas and Bessie, then to Johnnie and Cate.

A head man made decisions, yes—but only with the support of his family.

But it was Stella who asked what must be asked. 'Cate?'

He held his breath. She had been wronged by the Storwicks most of all.

'To be sister to the woman who killed Scarred Willie?' Cate asked. She had learned to smile again. Johnnie had taught her. 'I could ask no higher honour.'

Surrounded by a smiling family. Life offered nothing better.

Stella looked across the field at her family. 'Shall we invite them to the wedding feast?'

Rob smiled. 'If you'll help Bessie fix it, love.'

The Storwicks were invited to the feast. More than that: they came.

Rob heard that Stella's mother, finally, had brought the rest around. She told them, and he wished he'd been there to see it, that the same angel who had saved Stella from the well had released her from the hut and revealed to her in a vision that her daughter had been saved for exactly this reason: to join with the Brunsons and ally the two families. There was more to the story than that, Stella said. She promised to tell him some day if he promised never to repeat it. She said he'd like it.

But it seemed her mother had decided it was miracle enough that her daughter would bring peace between the two families.

At least, peace enough that the shepherds would not lie awake each night listening for hoofbeats.

He sipped his ale, observing the awkward attempts at conversation. Rob himself was a man of few words under the best of circumstances. Even less to be said to a Storwick. But the women, he noticed, had no such difficulty. A few sips of ale and they started chattering like corbies.

It was too soon to merge the two families, of course. First, he'd get them to stop throwing spears his way. Later, when Stella's babe came, there might be something more. Later, when they realised the Storwick family would need a new head man—and who it should be—maybe they would come to believe, in time, that God had saved her for this.

Would his father have approved? Or hers? It didn't matter. Rob Brunson was the head man now, for good or ill.

Wat, who had never seen such excitement, ran round the room with happy shrieks, Stella chasing him as if he were her own. Well, soon, he vowed, she would have all the children she could chase.

The Storwicks, he noted, to their credit, were kind to the lad. Well, some said being touched made one closer to God.

They did, he noticed, steer clear of Belde. Cate's dog stayed closer to her than usual, overwhelmed, perhaps, by the stench of too many Storwicks in one room. Johnnie might be her husband, but the beast had never relinquished responsibility for her.

Rob lifted his voice, finally, after the dancing was done. Bessie and Thomas danced as well as Rob sang. They'd even persuaded Rob to take a step or two with Stella, though his father always said Brunsons did not dance.

Perhaps his father had been wrong.

Still, Rob sang better than he danced. And that night, they sang all the Brunson tunes. The one about the dog, the one about Bessie going to court, and finally, the Brunson Ballad, all the countless verses of it.

He even sang the one he had written for Hobbes Storwick, happy to raise a toast to the man along with his kin.

'I've a new song tonight,' he said, 'in honour of this day.'

A Brunson man is tall and strong
And stubborn as the day is long
But one was lost and now he's found
By the Storwick woman, come around

Brunson and Storwick applauded together when he was done.

'I think that's what happened,' Stella whispered, much later, when they were alone in the head man's bed. 'I think the Lost Storwick was the one who saved the First Brunson.'

He smiled. Still fanciful, sometimes, his Stella was. 'Maybe.'

'Well, someone did. He didn't just rise from the dead.'

'I suppose,' he said. 'Although he might have

been the man who found her. After all, they called her Leitakona. That means the woman who both sought and found.'

She was beaming again. 'And then she was lost no more.'

* * * * *

Author's Afterword

This book concludes the stories of the Brunson family. And it brings me, finally, to the incident that inspired the entire series.

As I've tried to show, the history of the Borders, real or imagined, is carried by its ballads. And one of the most famous of them is 'The Ballad of Johnnie Armstrong'. It tells the story of the time King James V came to the Borders to prove he could, indeed, keep order in his own kingdom.

From what we can tell of the truth, Johnnie Armstrong, or Johnnie of Gilnocke, was one of the most notorious raiders on the Borders. And to the local people he had preyed upon, bringing the man to justice might have been a welcome relief. Indeed, a few years after, Sir David Lindsay, King James's in-house playwright, made mention of it in one of his productions.

But history is written—or rewritten—by the storytellers. And the composer of Johnnie's ballad saw it a bit differently. According to the ballad, Johnnie, the 'King of the Borders', was murdered when he was lured to a meeting with the King by a 'loving letter' that insisted he come unarmed.

He did, with forty retainers, dressed in their finest splendour to honour the King, whereupon the King called him a traitor. Armstrong begged for his life, and that of his men, offering the King all manner of gifts, including 'four-and-twenty milk-white steeds' if he were spared. His final offer was that the King should receive yearly rent, more accurately, the 'blackmail' from all dwellers in the area of the Borders where Johnnie held sway, 'Gilnockie to Newcastleton.'

Alas, to no avail. Seeing he was to die, Johnnie made an impassioned speech, claiming he had never harmed a Scot, but only the English—and so had served the King well.

It's hard to summon sympathy for the King in the ballad, so deceitful that he tricks his subject into a trap. The song also suggests the King was jealous of Johnnie's fine clothes, another less-than-admirable trait. As he realises he is to die, Johnnie says

I have asked grace at a graceless face,
But there is none for my men and me.

I would have kept the Border side
In spite of thy peers and thee.

So poor Johnnie and his men were hanged and lived no more. Neither, legend has it, did the trees from which they swung.

I wanted to rewrite the story. I wanted Johnnie Armstrong to have a happy ending.

And so rode my Brunsons.

There are parallels to truth in my tale. The Brunsons may remind some of the Armstrongs. Some aspects of Thomas Carwell's story were inspired by the Maxwell family, though my families are all imaginary.

King James, of course, is not. James V really did travel to the Borders during the summers of 1529 and 1530, trying desperately to restore order to what was the most lawless ground on the island. Some suggest he had something to prove to his uncle, King Henry VIII of England. You can trace James's itineraries and he did travel as far west as Dumfries, where Thomas Carwell lived.

But the rest, Brunsons, Storwicks and Carwell, never existed.

At least, I don't think they did. But on the Borders, it is not always easy to tell.